FERDINAND

Also by Munro Leaf
and
Illustrated by Robert Lawson

WEE GILLIS

The Story of
FERDINAND

By Munro Leaf
Illustrated by Robert Lawson

THE VIKING PRESS · PUBLISHERS

VIKING SEAFARER EDITION
ISSUED IN 1969 BY THE VIKING PRESS, INC.
625 MADISON AVENUE, NEW YORK, N.Y. 10022
DISTRIBUTED IN CANADA BY
THE MACMILLAN COMPANY OF CANADA LIMITED
LIBRARY OF CONGRESS CATALOG CARD NUMBER: 36-19452
PIC BK
PRINTED IN U.S.A.
SBN 670-05014-8

3   4   5   6   74   73   72   71

Once upon a time in Spain

there was a little bull and his
name was Ferdinand.

All the other little bulls he lived with would run and jump and butt their heads together,

but not Ferdinand.

He liked to sit just quietly and smell the flowers.

He had a favorite spot out in
the pasture under a cork tree.

It was his favorite tree and he would sit in its shade all day and smell the flowers.

Sometimes his mother, who was a cow, would worry about him. She was afraid he would be lonesome all by himself.

"Why don't you run and play with the other little bulls and skip and butt your head?" she would say.

But Ferdinand would shake his head. "I like it better here where I can sit just quietly and smell the flowers."

His mother saw that he was not lonesome, and because she was an understanding mother, even though she was a cow, she let him just sit there and be happy.

As the years went by Ferdinand grew and grew until he was very big and strong.

All the other bulls who had grown up with him in the same pasture would fight each other all day. They would butt each other and stick each other with their horns. What they wanted most of all was to be picked to fight at the bull fights in Madrid.

But not Ferdinand—he still liked to sit just quietly under the cork tree and smell the flowers.

One day five men came in very funny hats to pick the biggest, fastest, roughest bull to fight in the bull fights in Madrid.

All the other bulls ran around snorting and butting, leaping and jumping so the men would think that they were very very strong and fierce and pick them.

Ferdinand knew that they wouldn't pick him and he didn't care. So he went out to his favorite cork tree to sit down.

He didn't look where he was sitting and instead of sitting on the nice cool grass in the shade he sat on a bumble bee.

Well, if you were a bumble bee and a bull sat on you what would you do? You would sting him. And that is just what this bee did to Ferdinand.

Wow! Did it hurt! Ferdinand jumped up with a snort. He ran around puffing and snorting, butting and pawing the ground as if he were crazy.

RL

The five men saw him and they all shouted with joy. Here was the largest and fiercest bull of all. Just the one for the bull fights in Madrid!

So they took him away for the
bull fight day in a cart.

To MADRID

RL

What a day it was! Flags were
flying, bands were playing . . .

and all the lovely ladies had flowers in their hair.

They had a parade into the bull ring.

First came the Banderilleros
with long sharp pins with
ribbons on them to stick in
the bull and make him mad.

Next came the Picadores who rode skinny horses and they had long spears to stick in the bull and make him madder.

Then came the Matador, the proudest of all—he thought he was very handsome, and bowed to the ladies. He had a red cape and a sword and was supposed to stick the bull last of all.

Then came the bull, and you
know who that was don't you?

—FERDINAND.

They called him Ferdinand the Fierce and all the Banderilleros were afraid of him and the Picadores were afraid of him and the Matador was scared stiff.

Ferdinand ran to the middle of the ring and everyone shout- ed and clapped because they thought he was going to fight fiercely and butt and snort and stick his horns around.

But not Ferdinand. When he got to the middle of the ring he saw the flowers in all the lovely ladies' hair and he just sat down quietly and smelled.

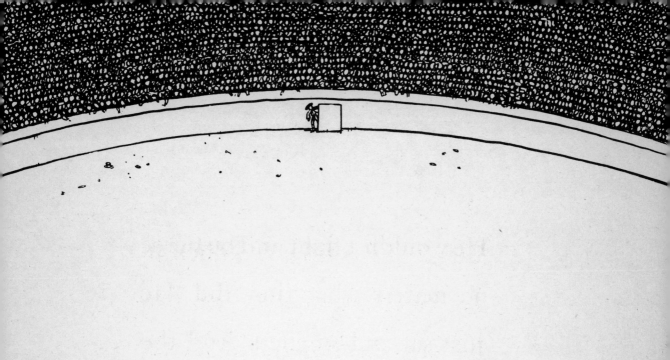

He wouldn't fight and be fierce no matter what they did. He just sat and smelled. And the Banderilleros were mad and the Picadores were madder and the Matador was so mad he cried because he couldn't show off with his cape and sword.

So they had to take Ferdinand home.

And for all I know he is sitting there still, under his favorite cork tree, smelling the flowers just quietly.

He is very happy.

THE END

BIBLIOTECA DE LA IMAGINACIÓN

ARAÑAS
peligrosas

Arañas
café

Eric Ethan

Gareth Stevens Publishing
A WORLD ALMANAC EDUCATION GROUP COMPANY

Please visit our web site at: www.garethstevens.com
For a free color catalog describing Gareth Stevens Publishing's
list of high-quality books and multimedia programs,
call 1-800-542-2595 (USA) or 1-800-387-3178 (Canada).
Gareth Stevens Publishing's fax: (414) 332-3567.

Library of Congress Cataloging-in-Publication Data available upon request from publisher.
Fax (414) 336-0157 for the attention of the Publishing Records Department.

ISBN 0-8368-3773-8

First published in 2004 by
Gareth Stevens Publishing
A World Almanac Education Group Company
330 West Olive Street, Suite 100
Milwaukee, WI 53212 USA

Text: Eric Ethan
Cover design and page layout: Scott M. Krall
Text editor: Susan Ashley
Series editor: Dorothy L. Gibbs
Picture research: Todtri Book Publishers
Translation: Tatiana Acosta and Guillermo Gutiérrez

Photo credits: Cover © Gary W. Sargent; pp. 5, 13 © James E. Gerholdt; pp. 7, 9, 11, 15, 17
© Rick Vetter; p. 19 © SIU/Visuals Unlimited; p. 21 © Rob & Ann Simpson

Printed in the United States of America

1 2 3 4 5 6 7 8 9 07 06 05 04 03

**Portada: La araña café es muy tímida.
Entre sus escondites favoritos se encuentran
las pilas de madera, las piedras y las hojas.**

CONTENIDO

Las palabras del glosario van en **negrita** la primera vez que
aparecen en el texto.

LAS ARAÑAS CAFÉ

Hay quienes piensan que para que una araña sea peligrosa tiene que ser **agresiva**. ¡No es ése el caso de la araña café! Aunque es muy **tímida**, esta araña es una de las más peligrosas de Estados Unidos. Su **veneno** puede hacer que una persona se ponga muy enferma. Algunos han llegado a morir por su picadura.

Por suerte, las arañas café no son muy agresivas. Pasan escondidas la mayor parte del tiempo. Incluso cuando se sienten amenazadas, por lo general prefieren huir. Normalmente, una araña café sólo pica si se siente acorralada y sin posibilidad de escapar.

Como todas las arañas, la araña café tiene ocho patas y su cuerpo está dividido en dos partes. Todas sus patas están en la parte delantera de su cuerpo.

SU ASPECTO

Una hembra adulta de araña café tiene, aproximadamente, el tamaño de una moneda de 25 centavos. Un macho adulto sólo mide la mitad. Unos finos pelillos cubren el cuerpo y las patas tanto de los machos como de las hembras.

A pesar de su nombre, el color de estas arañas varía de un tono tostado a un café oscuro. Machos y hembras tienen en la parte delantera del cuerpo una marca café oscura con forma de violín. Por esa razón, también se las conoce como "arañas violín".

Otro método usado por los científicos para identificarlas es contar sus ojos. La mayoría de las arañas tienen ocho ojos, pero las arañas café sólo tienen seis.

Los seis ojos de una araña café, en la parte delantera de su cuerpo, parecen tres pares de puntos con un borde negro dispuestos en semicírculo.

SU DESARROLLO

Una araña café comienza su vida como un diminuto huevo de color blanco. La hembra pone unos cuarenta huevos cada vez. En el curso de su vida, que dura unos dos años, llegará a poner hasta trescientos huevos.

Las hembras ponen la mayoría de sus huevos entre mayo y agosto. Envuelven los huevos en bolas, o sacos, de seda y cuelgan los sacos en sus telarañas, donde los vigilan hasta que los huevos están listos para abrirse. Si hace calor, los huevos suelen abrirse en entre tres y cinco semanas. Los sacos de huevos que se ponen en el otoño, cuando el aire es más frío, pueden no abrirse hasta la llegada del buen tiempo en la primavera siguiente.

Los hilos de seda que forman el saco de huevos de una araña café no están apretados, así que es fácil ver los huevos en el interior.

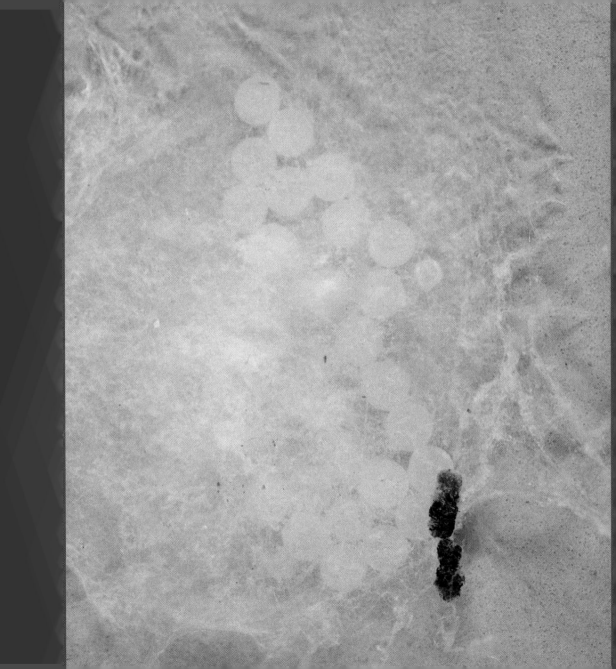

Cuando salen del saco de huevos, las crías de araña café no están aún plenamente desarrolladas. Para alcanzar su tamaño adulto necesitan entre diez y doce meses. A partir de ese momento pueden vivir otro año más.

Para crecer, una araña café tiene que pasar por un proceso llamado **muda**. Como las demás arañas, la araña café tiene una envoltura o **caparazón** que recubre su cuerpo. A medida que la araña crece, esa envoltura se le va quedando pequeña. Entonces la envoltura se abre, y la araña sale. Poco a poco, se va formando una nueva envoltura que cubre el cuerpo de la araña. Las crías pasan por muchas mudas antes de hacerse adultas.

Cuando una araña café muda su duro caparazón, éste se rompe en dos para que la araña pueda salir. El animal abandona el caparazón roto.

DÓNDE VIVEN

Las arañas café viven, sobre todo, en la parte central del sur de Estados Unidos. Su territorio se extiende, de norte a sur, desde el sur de Iowa hasta Louisiana. De este a oeste, es posible encontrarlas desde Kentucky hasta Oklahoma.

Estas arañas prefieren los lugares tranquilos y protegidos. Al aire libre, tejen sus telarañas bajo rocas o en pilas de madera. En interiores, se las suele encontrar en sótanos o armarios, dentro de cajas o debajo de los muebles. Algunas veces se esconden hasta en los cajones de las cómodas. A las arañas café les gustan las casas habitadas porque son lugares cálidos y secos, que son las condiciones que prefieren.

El cuerpo de esta araña café es café claro, y sus patas son café oscuras. Estos colores le permiten confundirse con su medio boscoso.

SUS TELARAÑAS

La telaraña de la araña café es pequeña, flexible e irregular. Está hecha con hilos de seda que la araña produce. La seda sale de unas pequeñas aberturas llamadas **hileras**, situadas en la parte trasera del **abdomen** de la araña.

A diferencia de algunas arañas que usan sus telarañas para conseguir comida, las arañas café las usan como refugio. Durante el día, prefieren permanecer ocultas, y sus telarañas son lugares seguros. También son buenos lugares donde guardar los huevos. La hembra de araña café no suele abandonar su telaraña cuando está vigilando los sacos de huevos.

La telaraña de una araña café es de un tipo conocido como "telaraña de lámina". En ella, los hilos están tejidos de manera irregular formando una capa lisa, como una manta.

EN BUSCA DE COMIDA

Cuando una araña café tiene hambre, ¡sale a buscar comida! No se queda en casa esperando que algo quede atrapado en su telaraña. Esta araña es **nocturna,** lo que significa que deja su escondite por la noche y va a buscar alimento.

A las arañas café les gusta comer insectos, especialmente cucarachas. Cuando una ve algo comestible, actúa con rapidez: primero, se **abalanza** sobre la **presa**, y después la muerde. Los **colmillos** de la araña **inyectan** un veneno que mata al insecto. Los colmillos, además, inyectan unos jugos especiales que convierten los tejidos del insecto en un líquido. Después, como hacen otras arañas, la araña café se "bebe" su comida.

Las arañas café son cazadoras y no usan su telaraña como una trampa, sino que salen a buscar comida. Esta araña café está devorando a un grillo.

SU PICADURA

Tanto la araña café macho como la hembra son venenosos. Su picadura puede ser peligrosa, especialmente para niños pequeños y para ancianos. La gravedad de la picadura depende de la cantidad de veneno inyectado y de la sensibilidad al veneno de la persona. Algunas personas ni siquiera se dan cuenta de que han sido picadas hasta pasadas unas horas. Para entonces, es probable que la zona que rodea la picadura esté roja e hinchada, porque el veneno de esta araña ataca los tejidos.

En la actualidad no existe un **antídoto** para las picaduras de araña café, pero los médicos disponen de otros tratamientos para aliviar los efectos del veneno.

A las personas sensibles al veneno de una araña café les salen unas llagas grandes y profundas que tardan meses en sanar.

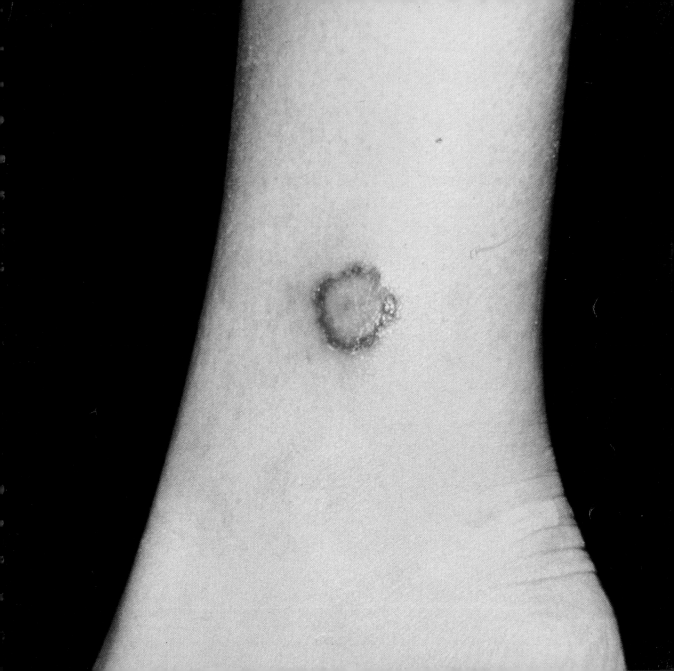

SUS ENEMIGOS

Pájaros, insectos y hasta otras arañas pueden atacar a la araña café, especialmente a las crías. Muchas crías mueren antes de la edad adulta. Pero el mayor enemigo de esta araña son los seres humanos.

A la gente no le gusta compartir su casa con arañas peligrosas, así que matan a todas las que encuentran. Para eliminar a una araña café que haya decidido **residir** en una vivienda habitada se suelen usar productos químicos.

Si ves a una araña café en casa, es probable que haya más. El mejor momento para buscarlas es de noche, ¡pero nunca lo hagas sin llevar calzado!

AMPLÍA TUS CONOCIMIENTOS

Libros   *Asombrosas arañas*. Alexandra Parsons (Editorial Bruño)

El fascinante mundo de las arañas. Maria Àngels Julivert (Parramón Editores)

Las arañas. Robert Raven (Editorial Könemann)

Las arañas. Serie Investigate (Random House Australia)

Guía de Naturaleza: Insectos y arácnidos. (Editorial Blume)

Bichos, arañas y serpientes. Ken Preston-Mafham, Nigel Marven y Rob Harvey (LIBSA)

PÁGINAS WEB

Las páginas web cambian con frecuencia, y es posible que alguna de las que te recomendamos aquí ya no esté disponible. Para conseguir más información sobre las arañas café, puedes usar un buen buscador como **Yahooligans!** [**www.yahooligans.com**] o Google [**www.google.com**]. Aquí tienes algunas palabras clave que te pueden ayudar en la búsqueda: araña café, araña reclusa, arañas venenosas, picaduras de araña.

http://iibce.edu.uy/difusion/
Además de información sobre distintos tipos de arañas, esta página incluye fotografías y consejos para recolectar y criar estos animales. Está bien organizada y te resultará muy divertida.

http://www.geocities.com/SoHo/1700/ spider.html
Esta página usa un lenguaje un poco más técnico que otras, pero la información está bien organizada. Algunos de los temas que incluye son: estructura, seda, veneno y reproducción de las arañas.

http://www.people.virginia.edu/~nbm5b/ spiders/
En esta página puedes encontrar un diagrama de una araña y otros datos sobre estos animales, además de un archivo de fotos de arañas, un poema sobre las arañas y hasta una receta para hacer una araña de chocolate.

http://www2.texashealth.org/ESP/drtango/ healthcenters/childsafety/outdoor_safety/e ncy/brown%20recluse/brownrecluse.htm
Artículo de una serie que contiene información sobre la mordedura de la araña café, también conocida como araña reclusa parda. Explica cómo podemos evitar que nos pique esta araña, así como los síntomas de su mordedura y su tratamiento. Incluye una lista de preguntas frecuentes con sus respectivas respuestas.

GLOSARIO

Puedes encontrar estos términos en las páginas que aparecen tras cada definición. Leer la palabra dentro de una oración te ayudará a entenderla mejor.

abalanzarse — lanzarse por sorpresa sobre algo, por lo general para capturarlo 16

abdomen — parte trasera del cuerpo de una araña, en la que se encuentran las hileras, los huevos, el corazón, los pulmones y otros órganos 14

agresiva — atrevida y enérgica; que suele iniciar un ataque o pelea 4

antídoto — tipo de medicamento que impide que el veneno provoque dolor, enfermedades o la muerte 18

caparazón — recubrimiento duro que protege el cuerpo de un animal y sus órganos 10

colmillos — dientes largos y puntiagudos 16

hileras — órganos situados en la parte trasera del abdomen de una araña, que el animal usa para producir seda 14

inyectar — meter a presión un líquido en los tejidos corporales usando un objeto puntiagudo como una aguja 16, 18

muda — eliminación de una capa externa del cuerpo, como la piel, para que aparezca una nueva 10

nocturna — que está activa durante la noche y descansa durante el día 16

presa — animal que sirve de alimento a otro animal 16

residir — vivir en un lugar 20

tímida — llena de temor 4

veneno — sustancia tóxica que un animal produce en su cuerpo y que transmite a su víctima por medio de una picadura o mordedura 4, 16, 18

ÍNDICE

THE TASTE OF OUR TIME

Collection planned and directed by

ALBERT SKIRA

BIOGRAPHICAL AND CRITICAL STUDY
BY
EUGENIO BATTISTI

Translated from the Italian by James Emmons

GIOTTO

SKIRA

Title page:
Scenes from the Life of Joachim: The Annunciation to St Anne
(detail), 1305-1306. Fresco. Scrovegni Chapel, Padua.

✳

© by Editions d'Art Albert Skira, 1960.
Library of Congress Catalog Card Number: 60-8730.

✳

Distributed in the United States by
THE WORLD PUBLISHING COMPANY
2231 West 110th Street - Cleveland 2, Ohio

GIOTTO studies have reached a decisive turning point. A careful sifting of the available documents is now making it possible to establish a more satisfactory chronology of the artist's œuvre. Recent restorations of the Santa Croce frescos in Florence have yielded almost miraculous results. Cleared of 19th-century repainting, the frescos in the Bardi Chapel have revealed an unexpected freedom of handling and coloristic verve; those in the Peruzzi Chapel have confirmed the unprecedented monumentality so much admired in the High Renaissance. Many panel paintings too, by Giotto or his school, have been restored to something very like their original state. In the same way, with the work of cleaning now in progress, visitors to the Scrovegni Chapel in Padua will soon be able to appreciate unsuspected refinements of color in the frescos there.

We find ourselves, then, nearly seven hundred years after Giotto's birth, in the presence of a group of really admirable works, easily accessible, which modern techniques of reproduction enable us to compare in their minutest details, and which every tourist to Italy makes a point of seeing. Never has Giotto's fame been so great as it is now. Innumerable studies and monographs have been devoted to him, while technical analyses of his great fresco cycles have reached the stage where we can almost follow their development day by day, can almost fathom the master mind behind them, and even grasp the mainsprings of his craftsmanship as well as his artistry, the human side of the man as well as his genius.

Yet, for all this, Giotto remains profoundly enigmatic. Equally enigmatic remain the origins of monumental painting in Tuscany. The problems so far solved have given rise to a thousand others, which call for solution in turn. In the light of the authentic documents, not only the older interpretations of Giotto but even the most recent seem biased or out of date.

Our analytical method also contains an element of uncertainty. If we confine our study to autograph works, in which the artist's hand seems to have left its mark, then Giotto's world, already grievously diminished by so many losses, appears narrow indeed in view of the fame it enjoys and the impact it has had. If on the other hand we enlarge the field of scrutiny, we do so at the risk of losing any valid criterion of judgment. His pupils and imitators, the Trecento critics and his Renaissance admirers, all contributed to create what might be called the Giotto myth. And the historical importance of this myth is in a sense greater than that of Giotto himself. Like Cubism in our time, Giottism grew into a movement transcending any single personality, evolving in accordance with laws of its own.

This is true, however, not only of the greatest of Trecento painters, but of many masters of Italian art. One of the foremost architects, thinkers and men of taste of Renaissance times, Leon Battista Alberti, who in some ways resembled Giotto, remains something of a riddle as far as his own individuality goes, in spite of the thorough knowledge we have of his masterpieces. This is largely due to the fact that these great personalities left the execution of much of their work to pupils and assistants, or better, created, in addition to their own personal style, a collective style; they became the moving spirit of a whole society, and besides being artists were men of action. So that to confine ourselves to their autograph works amounts, in effect, to removing them bodily from a much larger historical and cultural context. But on the other hand, if we fail to go back

BIOGRAPHICAL RECORDS

WE have far more records and testimonies relating to Giotto than to any other earlier or contemporary artist. With him moreover begins art criticism, which at first, in imitation of the ancients, was mainly biographical. Giotto, in other words, was acknowledged to be as deserving of applause and commemoration as a great *condottiere* or a famous man of letters. The figurative arts, hitherto dismissed as mere handicrafts, became a humanist discipline thanks to him.

We find him described as a man of culture and learning, avid of glory. His works were recorded in town chronicles; such was the case at both Padua and Florence. He was spoken of with reverence by famous writers like Petrarch, Boccaccio and Francesco da Barberino. Dante mentions him. In Florence he was a national hero. The *novella* writers seized on him as a character well suited to enliven their tales, and put jokes and witticisms into his mouth; the picture they give is that of a shrewd and sturdy burgher, with a ready wit, at times of a rude and popular cast. Legends sprang up around his name, picturing him as a precocious genius, early surpassing his teacher, almost at once a recognized master. Even when we make allowance for some ingenuousness and the frequent use of stock phrases often derived from classical authors, the Trecento and Quattrocento documents that we have all agree in one particular: the extraordinary novelty of Giotto's style and the force of his personality. In time this impression crystallized in an outright assertion, to the effect that with Giotto the dead art of painting was resurrected and given a new lease of life. The most solemn expression of this idea is perhaps that given in 1440 by Aeneas Silvius Piccolomini (the future Pius II), who, much as Giotto's immediate contemporaries had done, associated the new flowering of painting and the arts with the renewal of letters and culture in general. "As literature fell into decay, so painting too declined. When the former recovered, the latter also lifted up its head. We have seen that for two hundred years painting had none of the refinements of art. The writings of that period are rude, inept, uncouth. After Petrarch letters revived. After Giotto the painter's hand regained its powers, and we have already seen both letters and painting attain the summit of art" (*Epistulae*, CXIX, Lugano 1518).

So Giotto, together with Petrarch, came to be regarded as the very founder of the Renaissance—an interpretation which, while certainly straining the facts of history, indicates the importance of his cultural even more than his artistic legacy. As for the masters who came after him, not only Masaccio and Donatello pored over his work, but so did Michelangelo, who extolled its expressive power. We today are more inclined to see the Trecento side of Giotto's art. And this shift of emphasis predisposes us to accuse the early critics of partiality, for by making an abstract idol of the real man, they quite ignored some of his most peculiar characteristics and fostered a confusion of attributions that increased with time. But our position, after all, is no doubt as biased as theirs.

Giotto's fame in his lifetime was also unusual in another respect, as even Dante seems to imply: he became a fashionable artist. Popes and princes vied for his services, at Padua, Naples, Milan, Rome. Already in his early works in Rome he conveys the impression of being a typical court painter. He owed his fame indeed to his outstanding abilities, but also to the fact that his taste coincided with the modern-minded, classicizing tendencies of the humanists of his day. As one of his distant followers, Cennino Cennini, said of him, "he translated the art of painting from Greek into Latin." With Giotto, then, Italy first acquired a truly national art, one which, moreover (though this view is historically indefensible), was regarded as a direct and spontaneous rebirth of antiquity: hence more universal, more legitimate than the Byzantine tradition. Giotto was thus credited with renewing the link with past glories that had been too long eclipsed, and with gathering in their heritage. What the *signorie*, as heirs of Rome, and above all the pope were trying to do politically, Giotto did far more successfully in art. He was accordingly regarded, down to the end of the 19th century and even beyond, as one of the great champions of Italian nationhood, and, together with Dante, as the supreme national hero. Art, for once, overshadowed politics.

Set forth below, with a few comments, are the known facts of Giotto's life:

1266. Probable date of his birth at Colle di Vespignano in the valley of the Mugello, a few miles north of Florence. His father, Bondone, who had already moved to Florence some years before, was a native of this locality, with which Giotto himself remained closely connected, later acquiring houses and land there. At Colle, or in the neighborhood, his wife, his sons (one of whom became prior of the church of San Martino) and three of his daughters came to live. The name Giotto is a diminutive, presumably of Angiolo, the name of his paternal grandfather.

After 1272. Enters the workshop of Cimabue in Florence, after this painter's return from Rome. It is not known for certain which of his master's works in Florence or elsewhere Giotto may have had a share in while still an apprentice.

About 1290. Paints for his parish church, Santa Maria Novella, in Florence, the large crucifix which now hangs in the sacristy. Marries Monna Cinta di Lapo del Pela, who bore him several sons and daughters.

1296-1297 (?). Commissioned by Fra Giovanni di Murro, new minister general of the Franciscans, to paint the fresco cycle devoted to St Francis in the Upper Church of San Francesco at Assisi. This work shows a certain familiarity with Roman culture and makes it likely that he had already been to Rome.

1298. Executes the mosaic known as the "Navicella," in the atrium of Old St Peter's in Rome, commissioned by Cardinal Jacopo Stefaneschi.

1300. Paints a fresco commemorating the proclamation of the Jubilee of 1300 by Pope Boniface VIII, in the loggia of the Lateran Basilica.

1301. Mentioned as being the owner of a house in Florence, near Santa Maria Novella. Presumably he had left Rome by now. The frescos and polyptych (now in the Uffizi) which he painted for the new Badia in Florence may date from this time.

From 1303 (?). Continues to work for the Franciscans, painting frescos (now lost) of the miracles of St Anthony of Padua in their church at Rimini, known today as the Tempio Malatestiano, and decorating the tomb of the same saint in the basilica of Sant'Antonio at Padua.

1304-1306. Frescos in the Scrovegni Chapel at Padua. He was certainly absent from Florence in 1305, as he is known to have leased his house for that year.

From 1307. Paintings on astrological themes in the great hall of the Palazzo della Ragione in Padua, on subjects supplied by the famous astrologer and physician Pietro d'Abano (now lost or repainted).

From 1311. Giotto seems now to have made his home in Florence, where his name occurs in different records as standing surety for a loan (which shows that he must have been fairly well off). Hires out a loom at a very high rate of payment. Buys and sells land in the Mugello. He becomes in time a wealthy landowner.

1313. Gives the power of attorney to a certain Benedetto, son of the late Pace, in order to recover some household articles he had left in Rome; which seems to indicate either that he intended to make a trip to Rome or, more probably, in view of the tragic economic plight of the city after the pope's removal to Avignon, that he had decided to discontinue whatever *pied-à-terre* he may have kept there.

After 1317. Paints, among many other works cited in early records, scenes from the life of St Francis in the Bardi Chapel in Santa Croce, Florence. Four chapels in this Franciscan church are mentioned as being frescoed by Giotto; only two of these decorations have survived. Also lost is the fresco representing the "Comune Rubato" in the Palazzo del Podestà (Bargello); this was one of the most important allegorical paintings of the period.

1327. Enrols along with Taddeo Gaddi, Bernardo Daddi and other painters in the guild of physicians and apothecaries, to which artists were only admitted from this date on.

1329-1333. Works in Naples at the court of Robert of Anjou, whose intimate friend and familiar he becomes. Among other things, he paints a series of famous men in the Castelnuovo, and decorates the palace chapel and the Castel dell'Uovo. None of these works has survived.

After 1330-before 1334. May have gone to Bologna to paint the altarpiece now in the Pinacoteca and to decorate a chapel in the Castello di Galliera.

1334. On April 12 he is appointed master of the works of the cathedral of Florence, succeeding Arnolfo di Cambio, and official architect of the city walls and fortifications. The foundation stone of the Campanile is laid on July 19, and the lower courses are built under Giotto's personal supervision.

1335-1336. Summoned to Milan by Azzone Visconti to execute a "Vana Gloria" with, around it, the "most illustrious ancient princes of the world," and perhaps some frescos in the palace church of San Gottardo (all lost).

1337 (January 8). After his return to Florence, dies at the age of seventy and is interred in the church of Santa Croce, in a humble tomb marked only by a plain marble plaque.

Of Giotto's family the few recorded facts we have are as follows. His father, Bondone, was still alive in 1305. A certain Martino, a blacksmith, may have been the painter's brother. Of Giotto's daughters three married in the Val di Mugello; another joined a religious sisterhood attached to Santa Maria Novella in Florence and died shortly after her father. One son, Francesco, who came of age in 1318, became prior of the church of San Martino at Colle; he looked after his father's affairs.

According to Ghiberti, his outstanding pupils were Stefano, Taddeo Gaddi, and Maso. But Giotto's direct influence extended to a much wider circle of artists. Wherever he worked he founded a local school of painting, very fine schools in many cases, which proved capable of developing characteristics of their own and sustaining them throughout the century.

GIOTTO AND HIS TIMES

GIOTTO AND SCULPTURE

To form a clear and equitable judgment of Giotto's work, we must begin by rectifying several misconceptions, due in part to the chauvinism of his Tuscan biographers, such as Vasari, and in part to insufficient knowledge of the historical realities of the age in which the great painter lived and worked. The most serious fallacy concerns the "absolute originality" of Giotto's style. Well known are the famous epitaph composed by Angelo Poliziano at the behest of Lorenzo di Medici (beginning "*Ille ego sum, per quam pictura extinta revixit...*") and the tribute of praise paid him shortly after his death by Boccaccio, according to whom Giotto "restored to the light that art which, for many centuries, through the mistaken ways of those who painted rather to charm the eyes of the ignorant than to gratify the intelligence of the wise, had lain in its grave."

Now the 13th century was rich in masterpieces. Very close in time to Giotto come the extraordinary achievements in sculpture of Nicola and Giovanni Pisano, and the masterpieces, equally fine, of the anonymous sculptors of Northern Europe, at Reims, Bamberg, Bourges and Naumburg, for example. Let us remember too the very close relations, often amounting to dependency on Giotto's part, between him and Arnolfo di Cambio. Giotto, it is true, rediscovered the plastic values of painting, gave an object lesson in concrete figurative power which thereafter remained fundamental for the whole of Italian art, and solved the problem of pictorial representation in a way that was altogether new. His scenes are not sketchy or allusive, but solid, tangible, tightly constructed, rigorous not only in the delineation, but in the expression and attitudes. But he could never have attained these qualities without the lessons sculpture taught him. As a painter, Giotto must have realized that his art had lagged behind that of the sculptors by nearly seventy years. He therefore joined the classicizing movement, almost certainly connected with the renewed patronage of the arts, which got under way about the third decade of the 13th century, and which in Italy coincided with the fabulous activities of Frederick II. With new times had come a new art, answering to a more modern conception of life, for which Byzantine painting and its dramatic expressionism could no longer provide an adequate language. So it was mainly in sculpture and architecture that the decisive transition was accomplished, all over Europe, from so-called medieval symbolism to what is usually styled Gothic naturalism, which in fact became the basis of all modern Western art up to Impressionism.

So-called Gothic naturalism had already reached maturity by the time Giotto appeared. Yet—and herein lies his greatness—he availed himself of the new style to express, in painting, a much wider range of themes and moods than any sculptor had done. Renaissance writers dwell on the universality of painting, on the painter's ability to capture and record every aspect of reality in his own idiom, while the limits of sculpture are admittedly narrower and its subject matter less varied. Painting very probably owes this universality largely to Giotto. From sculpture he took no more than the notion and the canons of plasticism, exercising great freedom as regards iconography and subject matter; he seldom based his work on specific ancient models, and even as compared with such great artists as Arnolfo di Cambio and Giovanni Pisano, he was much freer, much more imaginative. Rich with this plastic and pictorial experience, he attempted to reproduce every aspect of the external world, with results that in many cases set the standard for coming generations; but in doing so he consistently reshaped the trend toward naturalism, guiding it away from the accidental back to the exemplary. Boccaccio very rightly said of him: "He had so excellent a skill, that there was nothing in nature, mother of all things and agent of the ceaseless circling of the heavens, which he with stylus and pen and brush did not depict so very like to what it appeared, that many a time with his handiwork it came about that the eyes of men were led into error, taking for real what was only painted."

Already at Assisi fine details can be singled out which show how keen an observer Giotto was of flowers, trees, animals, landscapes, architecture, perspective effects, light and shade, human types and costume, all recorded with unparalleled lifelikeness. In his hands, notwithstanding the severely geometrical, idealizing structure of every scene, the stock repertory of symbols used by untold generations of artists for sacred episodes was straightway renewed. From now on the heroes of biblical and sacred history appeared on a real stage (anticipating the scenography of sacred plays), and a stage so well defined spatially as to locate the action in a fully developed architectonic and atmospheric setting. The result was impressive: the sacred scene, unexpectedly removed from the supernatural plane, was brought to earth, brought into the home, into daily life, almost as if to show that the gap between the sacred and profane was very slight. And if the sphere of the sacred appeared to shrink alarmingly from what it had been in the mystical vision of the Middle Ages, the sphere of the profane came to assume a dignity and gravity it had never known in any other period or civilization. When the Florentine humanists later described man as an earthly god, they may well have had the memory of Giotto's wonderful, untiring activity in mind, and his monumental figures in their mind's eye.

This new sense of reality is usually associated with Franciscan thought, and rightly so—but only within certain limits.

That Giotto was sincerely devoted to St Francis is proved by his christening one of his sons Francesco and one of his daughters Chiara; by the fact that much of his work, and much of the work of his school, was done at Assisi; and by the many commissions he received for paintings in Franciscan churches, at Rimini, Padua, Florence. Franciscan iconography was boldly renewed by Giotto and his followers. All this is indisputable.

Giotto, however, was not the painter of the rightful followers of St Francis, i.e. of the *poverelli*, the Zealots or Spirituals who regarded Rome as a sink of iniquity. Indeed, had the testament of the founder been observed, had the order maintained the original ideal of poverty, then very probably Giotto would never have been asked to decorate a Franciscan church. As late as 1279 the general chapter laid down the following policy: "Forasmuch as curious and unnecessary ornaments contravene the vow of poverty, we decree that the decoration of sacred edifices, in pictures, carvings, windows, columns and the like, should be strictly avoided." Frescos, sculpture and stained glass, then, were to be excluded from the churches of the order, as out of keeping with those principles of austerity which have been consistently observed to the present day by the Cistercians. It was only by violating the decrees of 1279 that the church of Assisi was able to become not only the most highly decorated basilica in Europe, but for a period of over fifty years probably the most fervent center of religious painting that Italy has ever known. And this flagrant breach of the Franciscan Rule must have aroused a wave of indignation, to judge by the long resistance of the Zealots of the order, outside Italy in particular, to every attempt at church decoration.

This is confirmed, furthermore, by the early iconography of Franciscan art. The life and miracles of St Francis illustrated, for example, in the panel of 1235 at Pescia are, for all their dramatic intensity, treated in a deliberately hieratic and symbolic spirit; and the attempt to heighten the emotional power of the scenes leads to schematizations and cadences which recall the rhythm of a Gregorian chant. The narrative unfolds, in other words, on lines which do not pretend to be lifelike and objective, but which lay emphasis on specific motifs, usually symbolic, at the expense of others; on, for example, the intentness with which the birds—perhaps an allusion to those of the Apocalypse—listen to the preaching of the saint; on the bleak and lonely landscape around the hermitage to which, like a biblical prophet, he loved to withdraw. Even in the face of the saint, who after all was a well-known contemporary, we find little concern on the artist's part to produce a recognizable likeness, but rather a dramatic insistence on his asceticism and saintliness.

Apart from the legend of the *poverello*, the only theme treated by the early Franciscan iconography, in common as a matter of fact with other orders, was that of the suffering Christ, with the Virgin and St John at His side; a theme of the utmost pathos, perhaps of Benedictine origin, rendered with an almost paroxysmal linearism and expressionism. All this, moreover, is quite in keeping with the apocalyptic, messianic spirit of early Franciscanism. Today, with the famous poem of the "Praises of the Creatures" uppermost in our minds, we tend, in spite of ourselves, to view it in a romantic, or anyhow a Petrarchian, light. But undoubtedly the saint's invocations to all the creatures and elements of the earth are predominantly, if not exclusively, cosmological in meaning; and the structure of this same poem is wholly ritualistic.

In addition to this indirect evidence, we have a further token of Giotto's attitude, and one of considerable interest. This is a ballad against poverty, already attributed to him at a very early date; so that, even if not his own, it may be taken as being in substantial agreement with what were known to be his ideas. Poverty, to which the "party of relaxation" within the Franciscan order itself strenuously objected, was accused by Giotto of "extinguishing the good," of sullying the honor of ladies and maidens, of conducing to theft, violence and outrage. Those who advocate it are dismissed as hypocrites and rogues; the condition of poverty is not only unnatural to man, but corrupting, for as his song puts it, *"rade volte estremo è senza vizio"* (an extreme is seldom without vice). He goes on to compare a society founded on poverty to an edifice without foundations, and therefore unable to withstand wind and weather. The whole tone of the ballad is harsh and haughty; its arguments strike home. They proceed from a truly humanistic spirit, one that makes its appeal not only to the ethics of antiquity, for virtue, it seems to say, is not a mystical yearning but a logical norm, a middle way between two extremes; in this instance between avarice and poverty; between, socially speaking, an oligarchy of the wealthy and an absence of civil organization. It is certainly no accident that, in the allegorical series of Virtues in the Scrovegni Chapel at Padua, the only one to wear a crown, as queen of all the others, is Justice; for she does not repudiate earthly possessions but distributes them equally and stimulates social activities.

Obviously we are not to interpret this attitude as a form of selfishness, even if Giotto was a shrewd administrator of his property (he hired out looms at a high rental to workmen who were too poor to buy their own). What it does seem to reflect is a strong preference for the active as against the contemplative life, and in Giotto no misgivings, no moral doubts, are to be discerned. His confident optimism in the potential achievements of man—it is not for nothing that he was the first to paint picture cycles glorifying ancient heroes—went considerably beyond that partial revaluation of man and the world proposed by St Bonaventura even more explicitly than by St Bernard. For this Ulysses of painting the known world had ceased to be bounded by the pillars of Hercules.

GIOTTO AND DANTE

Since Dante too is held up as a champion of humanity, it was inevitable that he should be compared with Giotto, the more so as both were Florentines. The tradition of their friendship moreover, and even of a collaboration between them in devising the frescos in the Scrovegni Chapel, is a very old one. It rests on the famous comparison of Giotto with Cimabue in Canto XI of the Purgatorio:

> *Credette Cimabue nella pittura*
> *Tener lo campo, e ora ha Giotto il grido,*
> *Si che la fama di colui è oscura*
>
> (Cimabue thought to hold the field
> In painting, and now Giotto hath the cry,
> So that the fame of Cimabue is obscured),

and on the anecdote handed down by Benvenuto da Imola of a meeting at Padua between the painter, then a young man, and the poet. Then there is the fact that a few years after Giotto's death, his pupils included a portrait of Dante in some frescos they painted in the chapel of the Palazzo del Podestà in Florence. So the tradition seems to be well founded, and has accordingly led several times to comparisons between Giotto's frescos and the Divine Comedy, both from the iconographical point of view (with the disappointing conclusion that there is practically no connection between them) and from the stylistic point of view, in an effort to trace some affinity of taste between them.

Now while there can be no doubt that both Giotto and Dante consciously belonged to a new age, had a very similar grasp of reality, a similar rational-minded temper and outlook, a similar power of vivid representation, and lived in the same heroic climate, even where their religious convictions were concerned, the fact remains that, when all is said and done, the two men form a sharp and well-nigh irreconcilable contrast; a contrast that may readily be construed, assuming they actually met, as a party conflict.

That Giotto had ties with the theocratic party of Rome, or anyhow was favorably regarded by the higher echelons of the ecclesiastical hierarchy, is shown by the number and importance of the official commissions he received both in Rome and from the Conventual Franciscans, the monastic order most closely attached to the Roman pontificate at that time. Now Dante's hostility toward Pope Boniface VIII, protector of the Conventuals, is notorious, and this divergence could hardly have failed to affect the relations between the two great men. Signs of some such conflict can be detected in the Divine Comedy. The lines referring to Giotto are usually quoted out of their context, and so interpreted as a eulogy. But if we take the trouble to read the whole canto (which deals with the proud and arrogant), we realize that this so-called eulogy is far less complimentary than is commonly supposed. Dante by no means exalts the fame of the artists to whom he alludes, but laments the "empty glory of human powers," and the brevity of it, doomed to eclipse as new fashions succeed the old.

> *Non è il mondan romore altro ch'un fiato*
> *Di vento, ch'or vien quinci e or vien quindi,*
> *E muta nome perchè muta lato.*

> (Earthly fame is naught but a breath
> Of wind, which now cometh hence and now thence,
> And changeth name as it changeth direction.)

The only inference to be drawn from the famous passage in Canto XI is that, when Dante was composing the Purgatorio, Giotto's fame was already great; his name, presumably, was on everyone's lips. But Dante, as if deliberately taking the opposite view, publicly warned him against the sin of pride, citing him among the candidates for Purgatory, and insinuating that he in turn will be followed by others, who will behave toward him as he has behaved toward Cimabue. This, as it so happened, was never the case; the prophecy implied in Dante's lines was never fulfilled. These lines, then, though instrumental in securing Giotto's later fame, were not intended as a tribute of praise. Cimabue in fact was already dead when they were written; and, as Vasari suggested, the words *"Credette Cimabue nella pittura tener lo campo"* may be no more than a translation into the vernacular of the master's epitaph: *"Credidit ut Cimabos picturae castra tenere..."*

Even apart from this innuendo, which posterity misconstrued as praise, Dante, in keeping with his principles, showed himself bitterly hostile to the friends and patrons of Giotto. To Pope Boniface VIII first of all, to whom Giotto probably owed his reputation in the first instance, on the strength of the great works, commissioned by Boniface, on public view in the Lateran basilica and St Peter's. According to Dante, the apostle's tomb had been turned into a sewer, not only because the popes were guilty of simony but—as we infer from an allusion to the charges made against Boniface VIII by Philip the Fair of France —because they had revived idolatrous practices.

> *Fatto v'avete Dio d'oro e d'argento*
> *Che altro è da voi all'idolatre.*

> (You have made you a god of gold and silver,
> And wherein do you differ from the idolater?)

(Inferno, Canto XIX).

In connection with the Franciscans, Dante alludes again and again to the fundamental importance of poverty, thus siding with the party opposed to Giotto. For Dante, Poverty reigns supreme among the virtues and deserves to be crowned; we find in the Scrovegni Chapel, however, as noted, that Justice alone is crowned, the virtue not of the poor but of the powerful. There is not a word in Dante of St Anthony, whose exploits are celebrated by Giotto. Both the father of Enrico Scrovegni and two members of the order of Cavalieri Gaudenti, to which Enrico belonged, are relegated to hell by Dante; the first as a miser, the others as hypocrites. Many such examples might be cited; the contrast between the two great Florentines seems to be irreconcilable.

What about the visual world of the Divine Comedy? On the one hand, we find in the Inferno an interest in nature similar to that of Giotto, though stress is laid almost entirely on obscene, caricatural and erotic characteristics; in other words, on the "comic," as the term was then understood. On the other hand, as regards Dante's treatment of the divine, certain elements are symbolic and strictly aniconic. Divinity presents itself to him in the form of light, as three circles of three colors; light and pure color, moreover, play an emblematic role of prime importance throughout the poem, in which the poet's tremendous powers of plastic description are almost exclusively applied to human beings, or rather to the bestial and vicious side of human beings.

In a sense, this comparison of Giotto and Dante, presupposing as it must a conflict rather than any kinship between them, turns wholly to Giotto's advantage. He was the more earthbound, the less mystical, the less medieval of the two; he was the man of the modern age. And with him painting regained its prestige with respect to literature. Not only did it stand now on an equal footing of dignity with poetry, but it began materially adding to man's knowledge of the world with a vividness and anecdotal verve worthy in every way of the contemporary *novella*; and, in addition to this, with a dramatic sweep, an earnestness of narration and a sustained intensity of feeling such as to compensate amply for the absence of tragedy in the literature of that day.

GIOTTO AND SIENESE PAINTING

The contrast between the Florentine school, founded by Giotto, and the Sienese school is an acknowledged fact, repeatedly attested to by the early historians and sharpened by the political conflict between the two cities. At Siena, as the Middle Ages drew to a close, there occurred not a cultural revolution but a transition which succeeded in preserving intact not only a large part of the medieval subject matter, but also the old function of the devotional image. A Madonna by Simone Martini, though rich in natural undertones, remains evocative and symbolic; the devout who approach it are emotionally affected by suavely harmonizing colors, by sensuous, intricately weaving lines, by the merging of real space into an atmosphere, if not spiritualized, anyhow highly sophisticated. Florentine painting, on the other hand, in the person of Giotto, set out to express the logical character of the world in its very essence. The image thereby assumed a sacred significance, because constructed in accordance with the rules of the physical universe, and also became an expression of the supreme principles of reality. While a Sienese Madonna conformed to the canons of elegance, of refinement, of sensuality and overt eroticism laid down by the court poetry of the period, a Florentine Madonna was born of intellectual speculations in geometry, perspective and proportions; it was a product of philosophy and mathematics combined. It too of course was symbolic, and in a sense more openly so than its Sienese counterpart. But it failed to cast an immediate spell over the beholder; it compelled him, rather, to meditation and scrutiny by slow degrees, to a critical and rationalistic attitude. From Petrarch we learn that "ignorant" people were incapable of appreciating it.

Giotto and the Florentines clearly anticipated what was to be the most typical characteristic of the Renaissance: rationalism, self-control, the struggle of reason against feeling, even at the risk of neglecting many aspects of human psychology and of giving rise to an intellectualism which in the end largely discredited itself. However, Giotto's concern with naturalistic details remains, for all their novelty, a factor of secondary importance (as does his irrepressible fondness for decoration): his object was to reduce the multiplicity of appearances to their ideal principles. The Sienese, on the other hand, worshipped God in the very multiplicity of phenomena and in external refinements; they gave painting the richness of goldsmiths' work and stained glass; they sought to put it within the reach of all classes of society by making it humane, anecdotal, pleasant to look at; in every object and living thing they recognized a value, rightfully conferred on it by the very fact of its existence, and they made no distinctions of hierarchy between individual and individual, between object and object. Sienese painting anticipated, not the Italian Renaissance, but the Northern Renaissance and Flemish painting. In another sense, it may be defined as candidly Franciscan, for it retained something of St Francis's warm sense of humanity.

Needless to say, the contrast which undoubtedly existed between Florentines and Sienese must not be pressed too far; historically speaking, there was never a radical divergence. The truth is that in many ways the Sienese school developed under the influence of Giotto and his followers. Some of the Sienese masters, the Lorenzetti for instance (who after all had worked in Florence) and even Duccio in his *Virgin and Child* at Badia ad Isola, often come very close to Giotto. As against this, we find Bernardo Daddi, one of Giotto's direct pupils, sharing the taste of the Sienese to a remarkable degree. What is more important to note is that the contrast between Siena and Florence only made itself felt gradually, especially after the rise and triumph of Simone Martini, so that the differences between the two schools may also be regarded as the natural result of a (perhaps) common spiritual evolution. Giotto himself, and this is the most human side of him, seems as time went on to have outgrown the heroic spirit of his younger days, and if more of his work had survived we might have reached the conclusion that, just as he succeeded in giving rise to a Sienese school of painting in opposition to his own, so he succeeded in nourishing it with ideas and in taking suggestions from it. Here again Giotto revealed himself as a universal artist.

WORKS

*

EARLY PAINTINGS · THE ASSISI FRESCOS
ROMAN WORKS · THE PADUA FRESCOS
WORKS AFTER PADUA

EARLY PAINTINGS

O F Giotto's youth we know next to nothing, nor do the early writers indicate any works which show him collaborating, as was customary at the time, with an older master. This is probably due to the fact that he was nearing thirty before he made a name for himself with his Assisi frescos, and above all with the Navicella mosaic in St Peter's at Rome, which, located in the first church of Christendom, became his most celebrated work, while the early paintings in Florence must have passed almost unnoticed.

Early writers, especially Florentines, insist on making Giotto a pupil of Cimabue; there is no documentary authority for this, but such historical and stylistic evidence as we have tells in favor of it. Vasari would have us believe that, as a poor shepherd boy, Giotto attracted the attention of Cimabue, who found him in the fields drawing sheep on a stone slab. But this is a mere legend. Circumstantial evidence suggests that Giotto received a good education, including literary studies, Boccaccio tells us, perhaps in the school attached to Santa Maria Novella.

Equally meager is our information about Cimabue himself, who was in Rome in 1272 and so presumably returned to Florence with firsthand experience of the classicistic taste then prevailing in Roman art circles. Quite possibly he met Arnolfo di Cambio in Rome. Cimabue's instruction or example must have been of fundamental importance to Giotto, even though he resolutely diverged from him and pursued a course almost violently opposed to that of his master. Speaking of Cimabue two centuries later, Cristoforo Landino praised him as the first to grasp "the natural features and the true proportions, which the Greeks called symmetry, and the figures which are dead in the earlier painters, he brought to life in varied attitudes." Important to note here is the allusion to structural solidity, obtained by the geometric quadrature of figures, a method known to us chiefly through the notebook of a slightly earlier French architect: Villard de Honnecourt. That Cimabue was also a qualified architect is shown by his collaboration with Arnolfo, toward the end of his career, in building the new cathedral of Florence.

The only painting that evinces a close personal contact with Cimabue happens to be Giotto's earliest known work: the large crucifix in Santa Maria Novella, still archaic in some respects but already the work of a master. It was designed to be hung, in the middle of the vast Dominican church, on a choir-screen which was torn down in 1500. Santa Maria Novella was the first great Gothic church of Florence, and also the most austere. Giotto's dramatic, profoundly moving crucifix was thus inserted in a rigorously severe architectural complex unrelieved by any decoration, in accordance with the ascetic principles observed in early monastic churches.

The history of the church itself provides a few clues to the dating of Giotto's crucifix. Beginning in 1279 with the apse, the building of the church went ahead slowly; the façade was not begun till 1300. But as early as 1285 the confraternity of the "Laudesi" ordered a large panel painting for their chapel in the transept: this was the famous *Madonna Enthroned* by Duccio, now in the Uffizi. Since the choir-screen from which Giotto's crucifix was to hang belonged to a later stage of construction, his painting may be assigned to a somewhat later date, to about 1290; even though the earliest records referring to it only go back to 1312.

Both Duccio and Giotto had close ties with Cimabue. It was only natural for the Dominicans to apply to them when new paintings were required, for Cimabue had already worked for the order, for which he made one of his masterpieces: the solemn crucifix in San Domenico at Arezzo, undoubtedly

CRUCIFIX: THE VIRGIN, C. 1290. ON WOOD.
SANTA MARIA NOVELLA, FLORENCE.

CRUCIFIX: ST JOHN, C. 1290. ON WOOD.
SANTA MARIA NOVELLA, FLORENCE.

33

the prototype of Giotto's, just as Cimabue's graceful *Madonna* in Santa Maria dei Servi at Bologna is the prototype of Duccio's. Circumstances suggest that in 1285 Cimabue was again absent from Florence, and that the Dominicans thereupon applied to his workshop for the *Madonna* and the crucifix they required. However this may be, it is certainly a tribute to the courageous modernism of the order, whose cultural influence must have been all-powerful at that time, that its Florentine church should have housed two such masterpieces, one marking the point of departure of the Sienese school, the other of the Florentine Renaissance. Duccio and Giotto, whose paths apparently never crossed again, were then living in the same quarter of Florence, each subjecting Cimabue's style to a severe critique of his own. Duccio was a few years older than Giotto, and the curve of his evolution as a painter was less dramatic; it neither forges ahead nor slackens off, but pursues the even tenor of its way, never falling short of the best standards of craftsmanship, and whatever was novel in his work was always novel in the subtlest, most intimate way. In his hands the sacred figures of the past were humanized, as if by a natural process of metamorphosis and attunement to the times; their gaze lost the sharp and chilling scrutiny of the Byzantines, and a mellow benevolence spread through their forms and features; they entered now, as it were, into a serene and confident relationship with the beholder. And when a touch of hardness or sternness lingered in the linear definition of forms, it was smoothed and softened by delicately blending colors.

In Giotto, beginning with the crucifix in Santa Maria Novella, the process was reversed. With him the human was deified, owing not so much to lofty refinements of style as to solid and tangible construction, calculated to produce the most compelling impression of physical force and presence. Giotto's conception of divinity was a subjective and dramatic one. And while Duccio fell heir to almost the whole of Cimabue's spiritual legacy, Giotto, for his part, gave a definitive catharsis to the religious and mystical torments he inherited from the past, transposing them from the emotional plane to a plane of rational certitude. Take the two half-length figures of the Virgin and St John, one at each extremity of the Santa Maria Novella crucifix: for the old gesture of despair, with the head pressed on the hand under an unbearable, crushing weight of anguish, is substituted the stoic forbearance of one who, dominating his grief with philosophic thoughtfulness, imposes a check upon himself. The same is true of the figure of Christ which, instead of slumping heavily to one side, with the belly swollen out, contorted with pain, hangs vertically from the fragile arms in a natural attitude of serene abandon, patterned almost certainly on the sculpture of the Pisanos.

Seen from close at hand, the huge crucifix reveals a number of highly interesting details in which we catch Giotto, at a decisive moment, breaking away from Cimabue. Here and there he kept to his master's practice, as in the sharp, flat, geometrized folds of the drapery, which forms a noticeable contrast with the soft sheen of the flesh tints, in spite of the bold mottling of the Virgin's mantle, with its rose-colored highlights, and the vibrant blue and violet-pink reflections on St John's mantle. Christ's body is carefully built up not on rhythmic but on geometric lines, with curves avoided wherever possible. Yet, the effect is one of extreme *morbidezza*, a delicacy and mellowness due chiefly to a skillful handling of color: over the green shadows of the body play roseate gleams whose articulation and vivacity are still strong today, even though the colors have darkened considerably in the intervening centuries. And the warm chestnut-brown of the hair and the reddish stubble of the beard, in contrast with the thick greenish shadows around and above the face, form a kind of aureole, more effective in its way than the traditional gilded one. The explicit stylization and gilded hatchings of Byzantine art have given way to an implicit, occult composition, an art that withholds its secrets, or better, its expedients. Gold is used very sparingly, and though gilding was originally intended in several places, it was in the end applied, very incompletely, only in the drapery and the borders of garments.

One further detail of significance: the outstretched arms are represented in perspective, with an eye to the effect produced by being seen from below. The faithful, passing under the crucifix and looking up, must have had the impression of a real body on a real cross, with their Savior's hand, torn by the nails, turned palm downwards as if to let the precious blood trickle down drop by drop.

Almost certainly earlier than the Assisi frescos is another, little known panel painting by Giotto, unfortunately mutilated: the *Virgin and Child* in the small monastic church of San Giorgio alla Costa, beyond the Arno, in Florence. The figures originally appeared in a much more spacious setting, the panel as it stands having been drastically cut down on both sides and at the bottom. Everything that in the crucifix at Santa Maria Novella was still a bold attempt at innovation, however fine the result poetically, has here become a serene and faultless achievement. The composition is radically simplified, and to this end the small size of the angels powerfully contributes. The full-bodied, almost statuesque plasticity of the Virgin serves to enhance her perfectly natural attitude. Untroubled by even the faintest hint of emotion, her face is a flawless oval, seen slightly from the side in order to suggest volume and to lend the figure a character at once human and hieratic. Even though the schematization of the angels' faces and the gracefully looped ribbons in their hair still stem from Cimabue, the two artists now have virtually nothing in common. Giotto seems, rather, to be confessing his debt to some sculptor's workshop presided over by a pupil of Nicola Pisano, perhaps Arnolfo di Cambio. The clean-cut lines of the Virgin's eye-sockets might have been made, one feels, by a sculptor's chisel.

Certain elements, the Cosmatesque decoration of the throne for example, and faint echoes of Cavallini, suggest that Giotto had already come in contact with Roman culture. Still, these might have reached him at second hand. The more we study this altar painting, the more we realize how much of Giotto's future career is implied in it; the early works of few artists have proved so truly prophetic.

ST FRANCIS GIVING HIS MANTLE TO A POOR MAN (DETAIL), 1296-1297.
FRESCO, UPPER CHURCH OF SAN FRANCESCO, ASSISI.

THE ASSISI FRESCOS

WHEN Giotto was called in (again, perhaps, on the strength of his being Cimabue's pupil) to paint the great fresco cycle devoted to St Francis in the Upper Church of San Francesco at Assisi, commissioned by the minister general of the order, Giovanni di Murro, elected in 1296 with the support of Pope Boniface VIII, he had completed his training and was an acknowledged master in his own right. Sacred art had surmounted the grave crisis brought on by the opposition of the early Franciscans to painted decorations, and the period of stagnation marked by the pontificate of Celestine V was past.

One of the most notable aspects of the pontificate of Boniface VIII, who as soon as he was elected hastened to grant indulgences to Assisi, was his policy of reviving the ancient pomp and pageantry of Rome, and for this he depended heavily on the figurative arts. His patronage of the arts was of course dictated by political considerations, for the conflict between Pope and Emperor over the rights and sovereignty of each had flared up again. Boniface, ardently embarked on a program of reconstructing and embellishing the Eternal City, was determined to establish himself as the only legitimate heir to the ancient empire of the Caesars. He resumed the practice— condemned by his enemies as idolatry—of having his portrait displayed in towns conquered by the papal troops, as a tangible sign of his authority, thus shrewdly taking advantage both of the enormous prestige then attaching to works of art exhibited in public and of the magic powers of actual presence popularly attributed to sculpture. The plasticity and dramatic imperiousness of Giotto's figures, indebted even in his early Florentine works to the principles of Roman classicism, were undoubtedly linked with the current belief in the magic properties of sculptured idols.

ST FRANCIS GIVING HIS MANTLE TO A POOR MAN, 1296-1297.
FRESCO, UPPER CHURCH OF SAN FRANCESCO, ASSISI.

There is no documentary evidence to show that Giotto
visited Rome before going to Assisi, but very probably he did.
At any event, it is now known for certain that the luxurious
decoration of the Franciscan basilica at Assisi was patronized

and financed by Rome, and carried out in strict compliance with the stipulations of the Roman Curia; it was largely the work of painters active at Rome; and Giotto's pictorial style and taste are steeped in obvious echoes of Rome. There is an undeniable connection between the architectural settings in his paintings and the contemporary or slightly earlier buildings designed by the Cosmati and by Arnolfo di Cambio. He seemed to be fascinated by those strictly proportioned but supremely elegant structures in which the sense of measure and balance, Cistercian in origin, unites with the grace, refinement and restraint of the classical tradition. So it comes as no surprise to find two unmistakable allusions to classical models: the sculpturesque pair of horses in the *Vision of the Fiery Chariot*, derived from some bronze equestrian group, like the famous bronze horses on the open gallery over the narthex of St Mark's in Venice; and, in the *Ordeal by Fire*, the group of priests of the Sultan of Babylon, closely patterned on a tetramorph. But, curiously enough, these reminiscences of the antique evoke a remote past, and serve exclusively to characterize either a celestial apparition or an exotic land of the East. Other references to ancient statues, marble reliefs and sculptured ornaments abound in these frescos, but they are always evocative rather than archeologizing; they show a firsthand knowledge of the style of ancient art, but a total indifference to the iconographical concepts of Greco-Roman antiquity. Much more precise, however, is the repertory of ancient motifs (ship, lighthouse, fisherman, and god of the winds) in the Navicella mosaic of 1298 in St Peter's, so the Assisi frescos must be earlier. At Assisi Giotto was still using these reminders of the classical world for fanciful and dramatic purposes. His impression of the antiquities he had seen in Rome affected only the style, not the iconography; this enabled him, however, to embody, freely and imaginatively, the suggestions offered by the ancients.

42

Gi. 8

ST FRANCIS RENOUNCING THE WORLD (DETAIL), 1296-1297.
FRESCO, UPPER CHURCH OF SAN FRANCESCO, ASSISI.

To understand something of Giotto's intentions as he represented the events of St Francis's life, we must first of all note the use he made of this figurative repertory, which he had probably collected in his sketchbooks directly from nature. St Francis, as we learn from the biographies compiled by his immediate followers, freely chose to share the poverty and

◄ ST FRANCIS RENOUNCING THE WORLD (DETAIL), 1296-1297.
FRESCO, UPPER CHURCH OF SAN FRANCESCO, ASSISI.

hardships of the lowest classes of society and, by living humbly, to make poverty itself a moral quality. The events attending the life of humility he chose to lead took place, according to the early account—the *First Legend*—of Tommaso da Celano, in the bramble thickets of the Umbrian woods, in a wintry countryside devoid of shelter except for rude wayside inns. And while the beauties of nature are movingly hinted at, the idea of taking any delight in them is held at bay like a temptation of the devil. Indifference is shown to everything that comes under the heading of art or craftsmanship. The saint objected violently to the building of even the most modest convents, demolishing them with his own hands; instead of rebuilding abandoned churches, he merely patched them up.

Now in Giotto's frescos, from the very first scene (possibly not by his own hand, however), which has the Roman temple of Assisi in the background, St Francis appears in a setting that can only be described as monumental and aulic; relatively few scenes take place in the open country. The Cosmatesque repertory of architectural motifs, with its equivocal combination of ancient and modern, admirably serves to detach the episodes from the contemporary world, even while continually alluding to it, and to cushion the shock of the saint's poverty by evoking a remote and noble past.

This architectural setting is much more than a "stage property," for it plays what is in effect the leading role. It sets the mystical tone of the scenes; for example, when a voice comes from the crucifix of San Damiano and speaks to St Francis, our awareness of the miracle is heightened by the majestic ruins of the great basilica which fills the picture. It characterizes the background: the pontifical palaces, the magnificent triclinia of the Lateran, imperial courts, monastic chapter-houses. Even in the episodes of a bourgeois character, it qualifies the incident illustrated by lifting it from the secondary context, from the stormy background of communal life, and placing it in the current of contemporary political life. St Francis, in a word, was bodily assimilated to the highest social classes of his time, and made to seem what he never wished to be: an epic hero. And all this not by means of stylistic symbolism, but through an almost sunny clarity of exposition, which must have seemed extraordinarily lifelike at the time.

In the Padua frescos, once again, we find an abundant use of Cosmatesque elements, but with a substantial difference. The episodes illustrated at Padua were drawn from Holy Scripture and their architectural setting was designed to give them a historical character. The Assisi frescos dealt with a contemporary hero, and the setting had above all to make it clear that the *poverello* of Assisi was in reality a philosopher worthy of the ancients. This also accounts for the imaginative treatment of monuments which were familiar to everyone at the time, for example the church of Santa Chiara, which is given a splendid façade of inlaid marble, rivaling the one designed by Arnolfo for the cathedral of Florence—a background worthy of a king's funeral.

Turning from the backgrounds to the composition of individual scenes, and taking preferably the best of them, the least crowded and most spontaneously executed, we find the same monumentality and severity of expression. This novel method of composing could hardly be better described than in the following passage on classical rhetoric by Dionysius of Halicarnassus: "Such is the nature of austere composition. It requires that vocables should be firmly placed and set out, that they should take up strong positions, so that the lexical elements may be clearly seen and succeed one another at appropriate intervals separated by well-marked periods. No matter if frequent use is made of harsh, ill-sorted miscellanies, as in edifices built with squared stone, whose foundations

45

The rigorous structure governing all the scenes of the ▶
St Francis cycle is clearly brought out again in their
simulated architectural cornices, painted with a preci-
sion and command of perspective that is quite amazing.
As seen in photographs or with binoculars from the
floor below, the simulated cornices with consoles above
the scenes still succeed in deceiving the eye. This is the
first recorded instance of a strict application of
modern geometric perspective based on lines converg-
ing toward a single vanishing point. Giotto's contemporaries were therefore fully justified in praising him as
a master of perspective. An equally impressive example
of illusionism is to be found at Padua, in the simulated
chapels in *trompe-l'œil* painted with consummate skill
on either side of the large arch over the presbytery.

THE ORDEAL BY FIRE BEFORE THE SULTAN, DETAIL: PRIESTS OF THE SULTAN, 1296-1297. FRESCO, UPPER CHURCH OF SAN FRANCESCO, ASSISI.

ST FRANCIS IN ECSTASY, 1296-1297.
FRESCO, UPPER CHURCH OF SAN FRANCESCO, ASSISI.

so graceful and dainty, so delicately colored, which, like the first of the cycle (presumably repainted), are attributable to an independent-minded follower of Giotto, akin to the anonymous author of an altarpiece in the Uffizi with St Cecilia and scenes of her life.

On the whole, however, the changes and innovations that occur as the work progressed are accompanied by an increasingly modest pictorial quality and by an increasingly incoherent composition. It has not yet been possible to single out the work of Giotto's collaborators, some of whom were interesting personalities. But a new study of the problem by Millard Meiss has been announced, based on an exact tabulation by the restorer Leonetto Tintori of each day's work on each individual fresco. Stylistic analysis shows, however, not only that Giotto's assistants were fairly numerous, but that large areas of the wall space, including some of the most famous scenes, were left to them. Giotto, probably owing to the brief period of time allotted him for the work, must have limited his personal contribution to a number of the leading figures, in some cases painting no more than the heads, while supervising as long as possible the general progress of the frescos, touching up and correcting the finished parts, and of course supplying designs, sketches, advice and help of all kinds. Without his guiding hand the results would never have been what they are, particularly as regards the skilled and coherent perspective of the initial scenes. What appeared, then, to be a marked evolution of his personal style may more plausibly be construed as a kind of reaction on the part of his pupils, who, lacking the moral and dramatic intensity of their master, developed above all the naturalistic and narrative possibilities of the new style.

The problem of distinguishing between Giotto's autograph work and what was executed on his designs or sketches presupposes another problem, and one of no mean order: that of determining the organization of his studio workshop or *bottega*, whose magnitude and complexity has been compared to that of the building yards of the great cathedrals. We may see a little more clearly into the problem by analyzing several of the scenes. In *St Francis giving his Mantle to a Poor Man*, Giotto himself must have executed both figures and closely supervised the laying in of the landscape, whose oblique lines adroitly serve to isolate and focus attention on the figure of St Francis. No doubt he also supplied sketches for the fine view of an Umbrian hill-town and for the monastery perched on the opposite hill; but he evidently left their execution entirely to his assistants. In *St Francis renouncing the World*, the hands of assistants are perceptible in the secondary figures, but the architecture is beautifully executed. In the *Dream of Pope Innocent III*, doubts arise as to the two figures, fine though they are, dozing beside the Pope's bed, while in the *Sanctioning of the Rules of the Order* perhaps only the figures of St Francis and the Pope were actually painted by Giotto. Handled with exquisite taste and balance are the *Vision of the Fiery Chariot* and the *Vision of the Thrones*. In the *Expulsion of the Demons from Arezzo*, the lovely view of the walled town, minutely depicted down to the rusticated stonework and decorative sculptures, with an almost Flemish love of detail, is the work of assistants; so are the small figures passing through the gates. While the stylization of the infidels in the *Ordeal by Fire* is very fine indeed, even though based on canons foreign to the master's taste, the whole right side of the scene, with the Sultan and his courtiers, is singularly uninspired. Many hands of varying ability can be detected in *Christmas Night at Greccio*, a scene too crowded and discursive; perhaps only one or two of the leading figures are Giotto's. Here his conception, however, is faithfully followed in the elegant rendering of the ambo, the pulpit, and the choir-screen with a crucifix seen from behind, all shown in flawless

ST FRANCIS PREACHING TO THE BIRDS, 1296-1297.
FRESCO, UPPER CHURCH OF SAN FRANCESCO, ASSISI.

perspective. Striking in their homogeneity, even if the secondary
figures are the work of assistants, are the *Miracle of the Spring*
and *St Francis preaching to the Birds*. The *Death of the Knight
of Celano* conveys the impression of having been left unfinished;
St Francis alone, rising to his feet behind the beautifully spread

THE MIRACLE OF THE SPRING (DETAIL), 1296-1297.
FRESCO, UPPER CHURCH OF SAN FRANCESCO, ASSISI.

THE DEATH OF THE KNIGHT OF CELANO (DETAIL), 1296-1297
(LATER REPAINTED). FRESCO, UPPER CHURCH OF SAN FRANCESCO, ASSISI.

table, seems to be by Giotto; the rest is more like a paraphrase of his manner than a faithful execution of his ideas. The same is true of the next scene, but to an even more marked degree; for this reason, and owing also to the intense, highly refined colors, it seems to belong to the group formed by the last three scenes, which are not by Giotto. Largely autograph in all likelihood, even though entrusted in part to pupils, is the *Apparition at Arles*, with its lovely transitions of color in the habits of the monks; also the scene of *St Francis receiving the Stigmata*, the last which Giotto supervised and unquestionably one of the finest and most coherent. As for the rest, he may have laid down the broad lines to be followed, but his pupils were left to their own devices, though availing themselves of a good many of Giotto's ideas and cartoons. The architectural settings now play no more than a decorative, picturesque role, while figures are elongated and their contours softened and blurred.

To explain these changes we can only suppose that Giotto was suddenly called away by other work more important than the frescos at Assisi. This, very probably, was the commission given him about 1298 by Cardinal Jacopo Stefaneschi, at the behest of the pope himself, for the Navicella mosaic in St Peter's. At Assisi not only did he leave the St Francis cycle unfinished (laboriously completed by his pupils as noted above), but also the decorations on the inner wall of the façade; here only the medallion with the Virgin and Child between two angels is Giotto's work.

To sum up, then. At Assisi Giotto's presence is felt above all in scenes with fewer figures; in those which were executed in fairly quick succession and thus betray no perceptible differences of manner. He seems to have executed personally—perhaps he was bound by contract to do so—only the leading figures, and carefully supervised the scenes which, iconographically, were most important. But as the work proceeded, his control over

THE APPARITION OF ST FRANCIS AT ARLES (DETAIL), 1296-1297.
FRESCO, UPPER CHURCH OF SAN FRANCESCO, ASSISI.

it lessened, finally disappearing altogether. Considering that the most confused und technically deficient group of frescos are those which come after the *Stigmata*, and in view of the controversy that raged before this miracle was officially recognized, it is by no means far-fetched to regard these theological difficulties as one possible reason for interrupting the work, which may not have been resumed till after 1304, the year in which the question was settled and the Church accepted the miracle of the Stigmata. But by this time Giotto was engaged elsewhere, and so the frescos were finished without him.

The presence of studio work, even in the scenes most closely supervised by Giotto, certainly detracts from the frescos; the style is in a sense roughened and hardened, and differs noticeably from that of his autograph works. Yet his assistants were anything but unskilled, and their archaizing style had one positive result. To the noble plasticity of the master they added a certain hardness of design which imparts to faces an element of religious transcendence. They thus pursued a traditional vision, as if the Middle Ages were not yet ended, and as if the new age of reason was not yet able to overcome the apocalyptic anguish and mysticism which had given Franciscanism its hold on the popular mind.

ROMAN WORKS

ALREADY at the end of the 13th century, Rome as it appeared to a visiting "tourist," as he rambled among impressive ruins, through fields still peopled with statues, with the guide to the "Mirabilia" in hand, and under the equally vivid impression of the new impetus then being given to architecture and the plastic arts, must have been very different from the image of the city that became typical for anyone who had lived there a long time. Even today those who visit Rome and those who live there take a fundamentally different attitude to the city. Antiquity, for the first, is an inspiration and an ideal; it is like recovering a patrimony of lost experience which one had unconsciously yearned for; like a re-immersion in an atmosphere of superior wisdom and, above all, of more generous morality with respect to the ideological restrictions of Christianity. But the enthusiasm of those who live there allows itself at length to be stifled by the weight of tradition and by indifference to any possibility of renewal. This is the Rome, rotten with millenary evils, which holds out no hope of any real solution, but aims always at a compromise between idealism and reality, between indulgence and severity.

Summoned to Rome to execute the Navicella mosaic, fresh from the burning atmosphere of Franciscanism, and plunged into the midst of the intrigues and cosmopolitan worldliness of the Roman Curia, did Giotto too feel the need to soften and smooth his style? Such would seem to have been the case, but no certitude is possible of course without the works actually done in Rome, and these, unfortunately, have nearly all disappeared. An inventory of the lost works, based on documentary evidence, forms an impressive list: the Navicella in the atrium of St Peter's, entirely restored; the frescos decorating the Loggia delle Benedizioni in the old basilica of the Lateran, of which only a fragment survives; various decorations, among them a *Virgin and Child*, all destroyed when Old St Peter's was torn down; other paintings described as *"pannus cum figuris Jotti inseratus et rotolatus,"* as *"imago manu Jotti in panno linteo posita in quodam ligno concavo,"* of which we can form no idea whatever; as for the polyptych in the Vatican Pinacoteca, commissioned by Cardinal Stefaneschi, it is almost entirely the work of pupils. With the help of literary sources and a few old copies, however, we can imagine what some of these were like.

The mosaic representing the ship (i.e. the "Navicella") of the Apostles caught in a storm on the Sea of Galilee (Matthew, xiv), with St Peter walking on the waters toward Christ, was for long Giotto's most celebrated work. According to a document published by Mancini in the 17th century, whose authenticity there is no reason to doubt, it was commissioned about 1298 by Cardinal Jacopo Stefaneschi, nephew of Pope Boniface VIII and a canon of St Peter's, with a view to attracting the attention of pilgrims, whose traditional practice it was, upon entering the atrium of the basilica, to turn to the east and kneel in adoration of the sun. This custom had already been denounced in a Bull issued by Pope Leo I in the 5th century; but evidently, though over eight hundred years had passed since then, this avatar of paganism had by no means disappeared. Shrewdly hitting on a realistic-minded solution, Cardinal Stefaneschi had the great mosaic put up, thereby converting the superstitious practice into an act of devotion.

Hence the location and unusual isolation of the work; a word now in explanation of its iconography. That it is meant to glorify the Roman Church is obvious: the storm-tossed ship, according to St Matthew, symbolizes the eternal struggle and eternal salvation of the Church and of those who seek shelter in its bosom. Yet, in view of the bitter political conflict then raging between Pope and Emperor, we realize that the Navicella mosaic

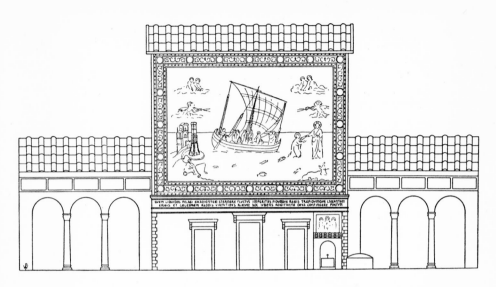

LOCATION OF THE "NAVICELLA" MOSAIC IN THE ATRIUM OF ST PETER'S.
(FROM THE DRAWING BY W. PAESELER)

very definitely re-echoes the polemics of the day. According to
a work written at the court of Boniface VIII, the storm threaten-
ing "not only the pope and the cardinals... but all the passengers
in the ship of the Church," was stirred up by the "multitude of
wild beasts," i.e. by the secular princes. The metaphor of the
ship, the "navicella," also occurs in the writings of those who
defended the imperial authority. Alexander of Roes had written
a few years before: "Just as the Roman eagle cannot fly with but
one wing, so too the little ship of St Peter cannot be steered
with a single oar through the tempests and whirlwinds of this
century." In other words, Emperor and Pope should join forces
for the moral guidance of humanity. Boniface himself, however,
saw things differently: a single "vicarius Christi" sufficed and

he was that man. And this was figuratively signified in Giotto's mosaic: St Peter's boat has but a single oar and it is held by St Paul, the Roman Apostle *par excellence*.

The impression produced by this powerfully realistic mosaic is attested by the following incident, among others. When St Catherine of Siena knelt at the foot of Giotto's "Navicella," at a time when both St Peter's and Rome (abandoned by the papacy for Avignon) had entered on a decline, at the thought that upon her alone had fallen the task of guiding the heavy oar of the ship of the Church, spasms ran through her limbs to which she remained subject for the rest of her life.

The Navicella must have been the work into which Giotto put the best of himself. Studying copies of it, in particular a 17th-century copy (Museo di San Pietro, Rome) reproducing it faithfully except for the figure of St Peter, apparently restored in the 16th century, one is struck by the parallel between Giotto and Roman and Christian antiquity. This, undoubtedly, was due in part to the intervention, probably fairly strenuous, of Cardinal Stefaneschi himself, one of the outstanding members of the cultural élite of the time, who was also closely connected with Cavallini. But naturally Giotto's own innovations are most striking of all: the use of vivid colors, still bright in spite of the unfortunate 17th-century recasting of the work; the many foreshortenings; the monumentality and plasticity of the composition. Early writers extol the variety of gestures, and their fine accordance with each personage and the dramatic part he plays in the episode; whereas the impression we get now is rather one of a certain confusion in the grouping of figures.

On the strength of a 17th-century epigraph, it is usually assumed that three mosaic medallions with half-length angels belonged to the Navicella. One of these was removed to the church of San Pietro at Boville Ernica, near Frosinone, while two remain at Rome in the Grotte Vaticane; one of the latter,

HALF-LENGTH ANGEL, 1298-1300. MOSAIC MEDALLION FROM ST PETER'S. GROTTE VATICANE, ROME.

unfortunately, has been altogether restored. But a 16th-century print shows that the decorative elements framing the Navicella mosaic consisted only of plant-forms. Were these medallions

POLYPTYCH FROM THE BADIA: ST JOHN (FRAGMENT), C. 1301-1302.
UFFIZI, FLORENCE.

POLYPTYCH FROM THE BADIA: ST BENEDICT (FRAGMENT), C. 1301-1302.
UFFIZI, FLORENCE.

then placed beneath the mosaic, beside an inscription? The most plausible hypothesis is that they figured on the inner wall of the façade, which was decorated with a band of similar medallions.

These medallions keep to the aulic classicism of the Navicella mosaic, though their plastic energy is less violent. Forcibly but serenely presented, the angels are distinguished by a certain Hellenizing grace, which suggests a firsthand knowledge not only of the painting of contemporary Rome, but of that of early medieval Rome.

Early sources mention, among other works executed for St Peter's, a cycle of five large-scale frescos in the apse. What appears to be a much repainted fragment of this (now in the Fiumi Collection, Assisi) was published by Adolfo and Lionello Venturi. It represents two half-length apostles with an unusual mildness of expression. There is something in common here, it seems to us, with the mood of lyrical melancholy pervading the Uffizi polyptych of about 1301-1302 which, as Procacci has shown, comes from the Badia in Florence. This too is a work of great mildness and refinement; the figure of the Virgin, though more monumental, anticipates the tenderest of Sienese icons.

Only a fragment survives of the last work executed by Giotto in Rome: the great fresco cycle for the loggia of St John Lateran, representing Boniface VIII promulgating the Jubilee of 1300, the baptism of Constantine (the Emperor submitting to the Pope!), and the founding of the Lateran basilica.

Again we have a courtly work intended to glorify the Church. The iconographic prototype of the central scene has been identified by C. Mitchell as a bas-relief representing the Emperor Theodosius in the tribune of his palace in Constantinople. Boniface VIII, portrayed in the act of promulgating the Jubilee, is meant to represent not so much a spiritual guide as the foremost political authority of the world, the rightful heir of those Emperors whose prerogatives he sought to revive.

He steps forward not merely to promulgate an act of clemency, but to proclaim a law worthy of eternal commemoration. And distinguishable among his audience is a crowned monarch. The overweening pride of the ambitious pontiff is seen again in the frequent repetition of the armorial bearings of his family.

It would be difficult to imagine a more solemn theme than this. Yet, judging by the extant autograph fragment and by Grimaldi's copy in color of the original, Giotto seems to have evaded the implications of the theme. His dramatic ardor has very noticeably cooled, as compared with what it was at Assisi. He tends to linger over details and anecdotal elements; so true is this that in the three central figures, Boniface VIII, the cleric holding up the roll, and the dignitary traditionally identified as Cardinal Caetani, what impresses itself upon us is not so much the ceremonious solemnity of the occasion as the shrewd characterization of facial features, carried to the point of sharply individualized portraits. The portrayal of the crowd below must have produced a dazzling effect, with its wealth of vivid colors and striking contrasts.

How are we to account for these changes of style? It is unfortunate that we still know so little of the Rome of that day, which must have been an extremely stimulating melting pot of all the currents and cross-currents of contemporary art, both in and out of Italy. And if Philip the Fair came to Rome in search of the artists he needed in France, it is equally true that he brought French artists with him to Rome—the famous portraitist Etienne d'Auxerre, for example. The penetration of French literary culture, moreover, was such as to make itself felt in the domain of the figurative arts. Giotto's evolution certainly suggests that, even before Philip's humiliating triumph over the Pope at Anagni in 1303, the political-minded classicism of Boniface VIII had come to seem—in Giotto's eyes at least— a whimsical and anachronistic dream.

THE LAST JUDGMENT (FRAGMENT), 1304. FRESCO ON THE INNER WALL
OF THE FAÇADE, SCROVEGNI CHAPEL, PADUA.

THE PADUA FRESCOS

THE frescos in the Scrovegni Chapel at Padua are Giotto's next documented work, following his stay in Rome; they date, as we shall see, from 1304 to 1306. Nothing is known for certain of his activities or whereabouts in the intermediate years, but one or two inferences may be drawn.

Giotto must have left Rome in 1303 at the latest, perhaps as a result of the grave political disorders culminating in the tragic death of Boniface VIII in 1303; possibly he had already left the city by the end of 1300, when he finished the Jubilee fresco, and may then have returned for a time to Florence. In 1303 Giovanni di Murro, who had previously commissioned the Assisi frescos, returned to Italy from abroad and was appointed Bishop of Porto. It seems probable that, thanks to him, Giotto was again summoned by the Franciscans, not to Assisi, where there were disturbing repercussions of the Roman crisis, but to Rimini. There, in the Franciscan church which later, as renovated by Leon Battista Alberti, became the famous Tempio Malatestiano, he painted scenes of the life of St Anthony (now lost) and, almost certainly with his assistants, the great crucifix still preserved there. Then he went to Padua. Such, according to the chronicler Riccobaldo Ferrarese, is the sequence of Giotto's Franciscan cycles—Assisi, Rimini, Padua, and this seems plausible enough. The Rimini crucifix, above all in the molding, recently rediscovered by F. Zeri, still shows a close connection with the Roman art world, and in particular with the Stefaneschi polyptych (as does the School of Rimini, which sprang from Giotto). Then, very probably, Enrico Scrovegni took advantage of the presence of Giotto and his studio in Padua to entrust him with the decoration of the Arena Chapel.

Since the evolution of an artist's style depends not only on the force of his genius, but on the opportunities and working conditions offered him, it is only natural that the Padua frescos should differ very noticeably from those at Assisi and Rome, and even from the polyptych of the Florentine Badia, datable to immediately after his departure from Rome. Unfortunately no copy or sketch remains of the lost frescos at Rimini and in the Santo at Padua. So that we can only look to Paduan culture, and to reflections of it traceable in his work, for some explanation of the new development of Giotto's painting.

Because it adjoined the luxurious palace built by Enrico Scrovegni on the ruins of a Roman amphitheater, the Arena Chapel is usually assumed to have been his private chapel. But this is not quite the truth of the matter. Actually it served as the church of one of the principal religious orders of that day, the Cavalieri Gaudenti ("mirthful knights"), and was designed to accommodate their assemblies. Their refectory, partially filled in, still exists below ground level. Records dating back to 1277 mention legacies and gifts of money and material for the construction of the building. To Enrico Scrovegni, a knight of the order of the Gaudenti, goes the credit for initiating the work of construction on a large scale and seeing it through.

His own attitude is, in a sense, quite as ambiguous as that of the order to which he belonged, but it must have tallied by and large with Giotto's interpretation, on the walls of the chapel, of the lives of Christ and the Virgin.

Enrico was the son of Reginaldo Scrovegni, whom Dante consigned to the seventh circle of his Inferno as a usurer. As such, usury being a mortal sin, he was debarred from confession while living and from burial in consecrated ground when dead; and the Church as a rule was strict in these matters. The son, in these circumstances, had no right to inherit his father's estate. But in this case a compromise—the more necessary as the Scrovegnis were then very unpopular in Padua—was reached

THE LAST JUDGMENT, DETAIL: THE VIRGIN AND ANGELS, 1304.
FRESCO, SCROVEGNI CHAPEL, PADUA.

either by Reginaldo before his death (but then Dante would have had no reason to put him in Hell) or more probably by Enrico, thanks to his personal friendship with the future Benedict XI. The terms were hard: Enrico was bound to enter the lay order of the Cavalieri Gaudenti, which meant that he had to make over any illicit or ill-gotten gains, even if inherited, to the jurisdiction of the local bishop. He was further enjoined to renovate the Arena Chapel at his own expense, to distribute alms with the utmost largess, and to lead a retired life; but in exchange he was granted permission to build himself a fine palace and to inherit a substantial share of his father's estate.

It is difficult to say how far his contrition and piety as a church builder were sincere. There is evidence both for and against him. In his favor are the rather touching inscriptions (drawn up by Scrovegni himself) and his express desire to be interred in the church he had built, this perhaps to obviate any risk of the non-Christian burial that had befallen his father. Against him may be reckoned, first, the distrustful attitude of both the bishop and the Augustinians (i.e. the Eremitani), who were entrusted with the spiritual guidance of the Cavalieri Gaudenti, and therefore of Enrico Scrovegni too; secondly, the very splendor of the church itself, which seems to have been intended above all to glorify his own family; and lastly the personal vicissitudes of Scrovegni himself, who was shortly afterwards driven into exile at Venice by the implacable hatred of his fellow citizens. Scardeone, a local chronicler, accuses Enrico of being weak-willed, abject and incapable of defending his own wealth and property. The same equivocal behavior seems to have characterized the Cavalieri Gaudenti, who at that time had already lost sight of their original purpose of rooting out heresy, and whom Dante brands as hypocrites and misers, covetous and unjust. True, the members of this order (or rather those who were compelled to join it) ostensibly led a frugal life and renounced public office; but in actual practice they moved in the highest social circles (only aristocrats were admitted to the order) and finally came to form quite a powerful caste, capable of exerting a political influence beyond that of the factions.

A perusal of the documents relating to the Chapel and the order may help to clarify the evolution of Giotto's style at Padua.

In 1300, empowered to make use of his father's wealth for stipulated purposes, Enrico Scrovegni bought the ground on which the Roman Arena had stood, and prepared to build a palace and a chapel. For this he soon obtained permission from Bishop Ottobono dei Razzi and in March 1304 the chapel was dedicated to the Virgin. Had it been wholly completed by that date? We know that it had not; only the present nave was finished. This can be inferred from a petition of January 1305, in which the chapter of the Eremitani (whose duty it was, as we have said, to keep an eye on the Cavalieri Gaudenti) complained that Enrico Scrovegni was having a bell-tower built beside the new church, to the great prejudice of the friars, who thus stood in danger of losing their exclusive prerogative (and source of a steady income in the form of offerings) of publicly calling the faithful to worship. In their petition they make much of the fact that the permission granted Scrovegni provided only for a small church, a mere oratory, for himself, his wife, mother and family, with no provision for public worship; whereas now, in view of the new work getting under way, the edifice bade fair to become a large church. Besides the bell-tower, presumably, Scrovegni had a small portico added in front (torn down in the 19th century) and must have been planning an annex to the chapel, as may be deduced from the presence of a door on the righthand side, which had to be walled up before Giotto could paint the allegorical figure of Charity which now covers it. Neither bell-tower nor portico nor this door figures in the accurate and detailed picture of the chapel which we see in the fresco of the

Last Judgment on the inner wall of the facade, above the main entrance, showing young Scrovegni offering the chapel to the Virgin, accompanied by St John and an unspecified female saint.

Now while there can be no doubt that the protest of the Eremitani was directed against Scrovegni's decision to transform his private chapel into the mother church of the order to which he belonged (encouraged in this, apparently, by indulgences obtained in 1302 *"pro visitantibus ecclesiam"* and above all by the papal Bull of March 1, 1304), the fact remains that Giotto's pictured model of the chapel in the *Last Judgment* faithfully represents it as originally planned, without either bell-tower or portico; so this fresco must date from before January 1305. That the fresco decorations of the chapel were not only begun but pretty well advanced at that time is confirmed by another complaint lodged against Scrovegni by the Eremitani, charging him with "many things done for show, out of pride and self-interest, rather than for the glory and honor of God; things he is again doing and preparing to do, without the Bishop's permission." Architecturally, however, the chapel is simplicity itself. What is referred to here can only be Giotto's frescos; nor is it at all surprising, in view of the then prevailing hostility of the religious orders to paintings and decorations, to find them condemned out of hand as vain and superfluous. The most zealous faction of the Franciscan order, the so-called Spirituals, passed exactly the same judgment on the Assisi frescos. With the Padua frescos, then, Giotto not only renewed religious painting but restored it to its place in the office of divine worship. And again, as he had done at Rimini, he created a school.

A few other inferences can be drawn from these documents. As the Eremitani wielded a certain influence and were the authorized superiors of the Cavalieri Gaudenti, no doubt their protest was not lodged in vain. The Bishop must have remonstrated severely with Scrovegni, and while he did not go so far as

THE LAST JUDGMENT, DETAIL: HELL, 1304.
FRESCO, SCROVEGNI CHAPEL, PADUA.

to have the campanile dismantled (it is still visible in modern prints), he restrained Scrovegni's mania for building and evidently forbade him to enlarge on the original plans of the chapel or even to carry them out completely. In Giotto's pictured model of it, which otherwise reproduces all its parts exactly as they exist today, we find a projecting transept with tall windows (therefore not a sacristy). But the transept was never actually

THE LAST JUDGMENT, DETAIL: HELL, 1304.
FRESCO, SCROVEGNI CHAPEL, PADUA.

Gi. 2

THE LAST JUDGMENT, DETAIL: HELL, 1304.
FRESCO, SCROVEGNI CHAPEL, PADUA.

built. How keenly this was regretted is shown by the fact that
some compensation for it was sought and found in the shape of
two simulated side chapels, painted with the utmost realism, in
illusionist perspective, on either side of the great arch closing the
nave. The simulated chapels conform to the original building
plans, and their windows are of the same type; each chapel was
to have an altar and, as we see from the painted perspectives,
was to be frescoed, like the nave.

By order of the Bishop, then, the work was brought rapidly to a close, provisionally anyhow, and the church was officially consecrated on March 6, 1306. For the occasion Scrovegni received the loan of some tapestries from the basilica of St Mark's in Venice. Some part of the decoration must have been incomplete and these were needed to replace it. What had not yet been painted were evidently the scenes from the life of the Virgin, in the apse, which were not made till much later; that is, the *Death*, *Coronation* and *Assumption of the Virgin*. Indeed, though the Arena Chapel was dedicated to the Virgin, the scenes devoted to her form a very limited part of the whole and were relegated—except for those in the apse—to the upper tier. We get the distinct impression that the scenes from her life were only introduced as an expedient or afterthought. This impression deepens into a conviction when we observe that this cycle of scenes infringes on the lower part of the barrel vault and fails to fit coherently into a decorative system obviously planned before they were painted. There are inconsistencies in its iconography; it even happens that episodes of the same scene are repeated, as Arslan pointed out as far back as 1923.

This last observation clears up the chronology of the frescos. First of all, the master painted the *Last Judgment*, on the inner wall of the facade, finished well before January 1305, in which we see the model of the chapel as originally planned; by the same date the scenes of the life of Christ were already well advanced; then, when the Bishop's decision was announced, the work was hastily brought to a close for the time being, before the single apsidal chapel had been built. Now that it was forbidden to build the transept, where an immense wall space was to be reserved for a fresco cycle devoted to the Virgin and Joachim, Giotto was forced to add a few scenes of her life high up on the side walls of the nave, above the stories of Christ, and, as a last expedient, to add an *Annunciation* on the triumphal arch. It was then planned

Gi. 26

While a rich background or undercurrent of symbolism was set up in Cavallini's work by a majestic presentation and incisive linework, in Giotto's Assisi frescos by the monumental heroism of the figures, in Byzantine art by distortion and insistent rhythms, all this is lacking at Padua. With the result that the figures in the *Last Judgment* have a curious ambiguity, almost as if Giotto could not quite bring himself to believe in the transcendence of the divine. The repetition of faces and the distribution of the scene into well-marked zones, devoid now of any abstract rhythm to lend them dramatic tension or symbolic overtones, are seen for what they are: decorative expedients, often rather tedious. The only notable characteristic of these figures is, at best, their serene elegance. Yet their naturalism is not such as to transpose the scene, thus deprived of any sense of the sacred, to the earthly plane and humanize it.

The absence of any real dramatic sense is especially noticeable in the figures of the Damned, for all the extraordinary novelty of their naturalism, already Late Gothic in spirit; but at the same time they are curiously barren of human warmth. They fail to arouse either terror or sympathy. What they do reveal, however, is an anecdotal verve worthy of a great storyteller. Animated by strange moral principles, they seem at times to give violent expression to anticlerical sentiments, as in the episode of a bishop selling a false indulgence to a sinner. The alternately obscene and macabre incidents taking place in this inferno, so different from Dante's, mark the furthest limit of Giotto's naturalism. Yet there are thoroughly modern touches that come like glimpses of the future. The figure of the hanged man, with his belly torn open and his intestines spilling out, is an almost textual anticipation of the macabre taste and very worldly uneasiness of Pisanello. At times, on the other hand, we find combinations of images that almost smack of Surrealism, like the reclining female nude tormented by demons, in which the theme of lust combines with the Freudian theme of blood—in this case, the blood of Christ. This, perhaps, is the first real female nude in the history of European art, for ancient sculptures, of the Hermaphrodite type, were still to be used as models for such subjects for a long time to come. But this nude of Giotto's at Padua is undoubtedly based on a flesh-and-blood model; there is nothing literary about the current of eroticism that emanates from her.

This is not to say that these parts of the fresco are necessarily by Giotto's own hand. But the very fact that they are there proves that he sanctioned them.

What had been a defect in the *Last Judgment*, which called for an epic, apocalyptic tone, became an extraordinary lyrical quality in the scenes from the life of Christ. The figure of the Savior, at Padua, is sweetly and lyrically humanized; indeed, throughout the narration of his earthly life, each scene has a character of its own, idyllic, lyrical, moving or dramatic as the case may be. An unfailing cohesion of style and content is perhaps the supreme novelty of this fresco cycle. The sacred figures remain of course strongly idealized but, unlike those at Assisi, they are nevertheless imbued with a vibrant humanity. The events in which they take part unfold on a psychological plane parallel to that of daily life. And the ambiguity that dissipated the dramatic power of the *Last Judgment* here heightens it, for the co-existence in Christ of a psychology at once human and divine underlies the very theme of the Gospel. It might even be said that the spirit of the Padua frescos is peculiarly suited to the devotional outlook of the Latin peoples; incapable of arriving at a theological interpretation of the Gospel, and by its very nature debarred from attaining to the abstract idea of God, the Latin mind fixes on the humanity of the Son.

LIFE OF CHRIST: THE PRESENTATION IN THE TEMPLE (DETAIL), 1304-1305.
FRESCO, SCROVEGNI CHAPEL, PADUA.

Was Giotto's spiritual attitude, in these initial scenes, in part determined by his environment at the time? Probably it was. To my knowledge, no studies of the forms of worship peculiar to the Cavalieri Gaudenti exist, but we know that they emerged and developed in the lyrical climate of the late medieval *"laudi,"* the first examples of dramatic verse in the vulgar tongue of Italy and still closely connected with the liturgy. The name of the order ("mirthful knights") suggests a "courtly" type of worship, conditioned by the aristocratic world of Provençal poetry, with its equivocal combination of the erotic and the mystical. Even in the lyrics of Giotto's time, the knight's beloved is often likened to the Virgin, sometimes even identified with her; and always revered with expressions of devotion closely akin to those of Christian worship. Love is defined as a sacred cult, a path to the spiritual life. And, conversely, the cult of the Virgin assumes a tone of affectionate familiarity, taking place in a climate undisguisedly amorous which, while contributing to an accord far more intense and intimate than before between the devotional image and the worshipper, also deprives the divine of its hieratic and eschatological aspect. What we are accustomed to define as the mystical currents of the late Middle Ages are all, in reality, sharp psychological reactions against transcendence. One is reminded, in this context, of a sonnet in praise of his beloved by a contemporary of Giotto, Guido Cavalcanti, whom Boccaccio defined as a "natural philosopher," like Giotto, and whom he described as intent on seeking "to find if it might be that God is not." In the sonnet I have in mind (the one beginning *"Una figura della donna mia..."*), the poet's beloved is likened to a sacred image in Orsanmichele in a way that amounts to a total identification, for all the miracles described in the poem, divine or amatory, are the effect and result of a supreme force, Love.

This vein of courtly poetry, re-echoing medieval mysticism in its love of precious colors, its decorative richness, its otherworldly idealization, was exploited to the full a decade later by Simone Martini, to unsurpassable effect. But Giotto, instead of sublimating sacred figures, confined himself to softening and chastening them, and for the first time in the history of religious art brought them down to earth.

LIFE OF CHRIST: THE FLIGHT INTO EGYPT (DETAIL), 1304-1305.
FRESCO, SCROVEGNI CHAPEL, PADUA.

This is particularly noticeable in their attitudes and gestures;
these have nothing sacramental about them, but are patterned
on the habits of daily life, though rendered with a certain
reticence and solemnity. The question thus arises, to what
extent Giotto may have drawn on the sacred drama for his
transposition of the divine into terms of everyday life. In the
churchyard of the Arena Chapel (for, in spite of ecclesiastical

prohibition, public spectacles continued to be held throughout the Middle Ages at the same places where the ancients had held them) the Easter mystery of the Annunciation was acted each year. This, however, must have been a particularly elementary type of play, and in general the so-called *"laude,"* acted in the vernacular tongue, is considered to have been still in the

LIFE OF CHRIST: THE ENTRY INTO JERUSALEM (DETAIL), 1304-1305. FRESCO, SCROVEGNI CHAPEL, PADUA.

LIFE OF CHRIST: THE WASHING OF FEET (DETAIL), 1304-1305.
FRESCO, SCROVEGNI CHAPEL, PADUA.

embryonic state at that time. But magnificent pageants were being staged in Italian towns, at Padua in particular; and at Padua too Albertino Mussato, with his *Ecerinide*, was reviving classical tragedy.

A comparison of Giotto and Mussato would carry us too far afield here. Suffice it to say that, in addition to their common desire to give not symbolic but vividly realistic representations of historical, political and biblical episodes, they both developed a new and remarkable capacity for bringing out the opposing forces of the drama and for presenting it not in terms of a general rhetorical atmosphere, but as a concrete encounter or conflict of personalities. Even the diabolical protagonist of the *Ecerinide*, the tyrant Ezzelino da Romano, has heroic and sympathetic facets to his character. So in Giotto, even in the cruelest scenes where the offenders' guilt is abundantly plain (like the *Kiss of Judas*, the *Massacre of the Innocents*, *Christ driving the Traders from the Temple*), even here the guilty, the villains, are not reduced to masks or caricatures but are shrewdly characterized with a thoroughly human touch; so that the conflict between good and evil develops and gains momentum on a broad plane of real antagonism. The *Kiss of Judas*, in which good and evil come face to face with such poignant intensity, would probably never have been possible without the rebirth of tragedy by then well under way in literature. The whole cycle of Giotto's frescos at Padua is, in a very real sense, founded on a dialogue, on an exchange of sharp and significant glances, while the Assisi frescos were rather in the nature of a sublime monologue, even in the scenes in which the moral and political heads of the Church, St Francis and the Pope, come together.

So it may well have been the circles in which he moved at Padua that prompted Giotto to humanize his figures and to adopt a realistic representation based on dialogue. But there is

LIFE OF CHRIST: THE KISS OF JUDAS, 1304-1305.
FRESCO, SCROVEGNI CHAPEL, PADUA.

a further element of novelty here: the physical characterization
of the figures, which indeed seems to be increasingly emphasized
as the work proceeds. We find human types of the most extraordinary realism: the shepherds in the *Nativity*, the sibyl in the